# A. J.'s
# L. A.

# A. J.'s
# L. A.

## WHEN
## LOS ANGELES
## WAS VERY YOUNG
## 1849–1866

A NOVEL

VICTOR G. HADDOX

ALMOND ORCHARD PUBLICATIONS

Published by
**Almond Orchard Publications**
6520 Platt Avenue, #174
West Hills, CA 91307-3218
PalladiumEducation.com

Cover design by Michael O. Smith.

This is a work of fiction. Names, characters, businesses, places, events and incidents are either the products of the author's imagination or used in a fictitious manner. Any resemblance to actual persons, living or dead, or actual events is purely coincidental.

First published in 2006.

ISBN-13:     978-1-939408-25-9
ISBN-10:     1939408253

10 9 8 7 6 5 4 3 2

# Acknowledgements

This story began years ago with my departed aunts, Dorothy and Hilda, relating to me their family knowledge and personal interactions with AJ and his brothers, speaking about them in the present tense, interspersed with comments about their parents and grandparents living in the developing cities of Los Angeles and El Monte. Characters depicted in the novel and their actions were repeatedly discussed and later documented by newspaper and magazine articles over the years. Memorial Day visits to the Savannah Cemetery made the characters live; it is difficult to forget our forefathers when grass is clipped annually and flowers are placed around their gravestones while one speaks of their deeds in the present tense.

Our cousin, J. Daniel Mahar, family genealogist and historian, provided accurate family relationships and family history, even as to the great, great grandparents of the King Brothers. The majority of photographs came from his personal historical collection and all rights are maintained by him.

Researching as a reader at The Huntington Memorial Library for a year gave access to historical documents otherwise unobtainable, and William (Bill) Frank, curator of the Hispanic, Cartographic & Western Manuscripts provided information in response to specific inquiries. Researcher George Fogelson documented many of the historical premises of this book.

Frank Damon, President of Las Angelitas del Pueblo de Los Angeles

State Historical Monument, gave outstanding weekly lectures on early Los Angeles and California for three months as a training course for new docents, which literally placed the listener in the era of early statehood when Los Angeles was beginning its amazing history.

Mark Troy, screenwriter extraordinaire, reviewed the initial manuscript of six pages and guided the author to the final rewrite of 150 pages. Greg Bailey of Integrity Editorial Services, provided an extraordinary editorial review and reworking of the material, and thereafter, gave freely of his time and suggestions regarding publishing, and above all, positive thoughts regarding the book and to its author.

Many thanks to Michael O. Smith who composed the intriguing cover.

My wife, Susan, our three children, and my eldest son Jerry who provided psychological support throughout the work of two years. My son Alex solved all computer problems. Without them, there would be no book.

# My Father's Murderer

I kilt my first man at 15. It was a fair fight unlike when the murdering dog dry-gulched my dad, Sheriff Samuel King. A no-good cowboy, Micajah Johnson, bushwhacked my Pa the Sunday night of January 8, 1855. Earlier in the week, they had shot at each other on the Foothill Trail running through town, and Mica had run away. Pa let him go. He wasn't even worth chasing.

But then Mica got properly liquored up two nights later in the Monte, hid outside in the shadows of a drinkin house on Main Street and fired in the dark at my Pa's back as he walked by. Pa's horse pistol was found in his shoulder holster; he didn't know he was being shot at, and he hadn't had the chance to draw. Without even knowin Pa was dead, Mica jumped on his hoss and whupped him west on Main Street from the Plaza to the adjacent Sonora Town where all the wanted men hid. When he heard Pa had died, he right away galloped off to The Windy Pass, Tehachapi, about 130 miles north of Los Angeles, at the far end of the brush covered mountains.

I knew there was bad blood between Pa and the Johnsons but not to Mica who was not related to them. Pa had marked out the streets of Lexington when we arrived at Trail's End in early 1852 and had settled in the water rich Monte by the river. He had led our wagon train from Santa Fe, New Mexico, to the California end of The Old Spanish Trail at the San Gabriel River. The Johnson Party arrived at Trail's End six months later. Although Pa had already named the town Lexington, Captain

William Johnson tried to take credit for the name and township, again naming it Lexington, and even changing some streets and boundaries. Micajah arrived in Lexington on another wagon train about four months after the captain and immediately took up with him. I never met Micajah, even though there were only about 1,500 white people in Pueblo de los Angeles and Lexington.

We laid out Pa at our house the next night, and his many friends paid their respects. I spoke with the men privately, for although my brother Francis Marion was the eldest son, I was the man of the house by temperament and physical prowess. Our other brother, Samuel Houston, was a full two years behind me and was not so worldly wise although he was often a wild man.

I wanted to raise a posse or at least get the Los Angeles Rangers to hunt Johnson down. The men listened with respect until my mother, Martha Mee King, a lady from Chatta Farm, Tennessee, quietly said, "AJ is needed at home. I have five children to raise, and now there is no grown man."

After that, no one promised to help me; I couldn't even get The Monte Boys, our wild group of vigilantes, to ride with me after Micajah, and I had been on many a posse with them. I knew then I must do it alone, just as Pa always had. At 15, a kid can be thin-skinned if he is not considered a grown man. The honor and code of our family had to be upheld, and now the new City of Los Angeles and our Monte looked to me as the man of the house. We were a Southern family, and all family mattered, especially those who had been wrongfully killed.

I took Pa's gun off the mantel; it didn't belong there no-how, with the heat and the smoke from the fire. It was a .44 caliber, modern 1849 ball percussion revolver made by Mr. Colt-a heavy 4½-pound horse pistol that packed a wallop whether you shot a man or beat him with it. Pa had reworked its envelope and harness so that it no longer was carried attached to his saddle but was slung around his chest and shoulders. I took after him with big shoulders, a fair to middling barrel chest, and the big, strong wrists and forearms of the blacksmith and steer roper that were my trades. This weapon was made for a man with my strength and size, though I was but 15. Even at 14, I had been fully grown with a height of a little more than six feet; I was not a stripling but an experienced trail man, battle tested for years.

We three sons, Francis Marion King, Samuel Houston King and me, Andrew Jackson King, had performed men's work since we were old enough to sit astride a horse. We punched cows, branded the wild ones and made steers with our Bowie knives. But at night we returned to our house for learnin with our mother in front of the kitchen fire. On the trail, I learned to read the Blackstone I carried in my saddlebag. As we grew, we rode guard for our dad's trail wagons from dawn to dawn, fittin off Injuns and banditos long before we rode The Old Spanish Trail to Trail's End in '52.

When I say I kilt my first man at 15, I meant the first white man in a shootout. We boys counted as men when we were 12, and were full grown at 14, although we were still polite to our elders. We hired out as guards at 11 years, and later as guides to those tenderfeet who tried to make it past the horrors of the wilds and deserts to Northern Texas, even to California. We were young, but we had grown a pelt of sharp quills over thick leather hides, and the long hours of work had made our bones heavy and our muscles hard.

We honchoed 51 weary pilgrims and their wagons to Trails' End in Southern California at the San Gabriel River in 1852. Pa was the wagon master, and it was his train. Frank, Sam and I were trail guides and scouts and general honchos. Injuns attacked us twice, and banditos once. We lost no one, and even bought back two white women from the Injuns for five horses each. I had fought the world and won, even before I grew hair under my arms. But I sure wish that cowardly dog Micajah had died by Injun torture on the trail west, for then Pa would be alive.

I would get Micajah by myself. I would leave that night when the house was asleep. He already had a day's jump on me, and I had to follow a cold trail. I made my preparations silent like as soon as our guests left that evening. I made my simple lump; just a small sack of beans, some jerky and the makings of coffee for a two-week ride. I had never been to the Tehachapis but I knew where the pass was, even though there was no marked trail. I filled two burlap water skins before I went to sleep, 'cause the outside pump would cry out in the cold morning and the dogs would begin to bark and everyone would waken. I hung the loaded Dragoon in its covered holster on the peg above my saddle in the barn. I gave Star, a medium-sized horse with a big bottom, a full tub of oats and corn and cached an extra sack of feed for him on the floor behind the hay. I spread my bedroll on the hay in the barn loft by the open shuttered window. I slept on my back that night so the first light of the waning moon would waken me as it passed by the window. I knew it would be late in the night, as the full moon had happened more than a week ago.

After the moon passed its zenith and descended in the west, whispers of light edged into the hayloft across my eyes, wakening me instantly. Noiseless even in the new mown hay, I rolled an extra blanket into my bedroll and, on the outside, an extra ground cloth because of the cold, wet winter weather. I crawled on hands and knees to the ladder, around my brothers Sam and Frank. Even if there had been a watcher in the barn, I would have been neither seen nor heard. When I stood on the earth floor, I grabbed the saddle with my left hand, balancing its weight on my left hip along with my bedroll, lump and gun belt, and gathered two horse blankets with the extra blanket and ground cloth with my right. Resting the saddle's weight on my left hip, I carried it outside to the corral.

Star was easy to rouse and fortunately was silent during saddling and cinching. The extra horse blanket on his back would help prevent saddle soreness during the long ride, as well as provide him with a little extra warmth in the mountains. He didn't even twitch as I tied my rifle boot to his harness, slipped my Winchester into it, then tightly tied the old leather envelope for the horse pistol to the pommel so the Dragoon couldn't be thrown free. I wore Pa's empty shoulder holster on my left side, ready for an immediate transfer from the envelope if need be. It was already cold, and I wore my heaviest oilskin slicker over my waistcoat and jacket. There would be freezing rain and snow in the mountains, and both Star and I had to be prepared.

I needed to ride far and fast. Johnson had whupped and galloped his horse out of the town and disappeared north along the Foothill Trail towards Tehachapi Pass. I had to catch him on that long trail before he went to ground and hid with family or friends. I would get him and make him pay!

I rode westerly for 13 miles along the Camino Viejo from the Willows in the San Gabriel Mission area, crossing the Arroyo Seco near Charity Street, and approached the Plaza on Aliso Street. I continued west from the Plaza toward the Brea Tar Springs, walking Star through three recent Mexican land grants gifted by our family friend Pio Pico, the last Mexican governor. I rode through the beginning of La Nopalera-the cactus patch-until mid-morning, when I turned north through El Portozuelo-the little doorway-heading for Cahuenga Peak, and up over the Cahuenga Pass and past Campo de Cahuenga. My mother taught me it was here that General Andreas Pico signed the Treaty of Guadalupe Hidalgo on January 12, 1847, surrendering all of Alta California, as well as most of our southwestern United States, to General Fremont.

Once beyond the Indian village and over the steep and tortuous Cahuenga Pass, I increased the pace to a trot, north through the flat fertile valley. I wanted to overnight at the Mission San Fernando and give Star a night's rest before I headed off to the pathless hills. It was also my last chance to obtain a real cooked meal.

I had never been to the mission and I wanted to meet the good padres who sent out their rescue team and saved the Manley-Bennett Party from certain death in '49 in Amargosa Desert, starving and dying of thirst. The survivors called that part of the desert Death Valley, and I had heard that name repeated ever since. I certainly didn't want to end up there.

The Mission San Fernando Rey de Espana was a hard day's ride from my El Pueblo de la Reyna de los Angeles, which was now called The City of Los Angeles. The contrast of the real Los Angeles, the Pueblo Diablo with its daily killings, to the bucolic surroundings of the mission was the journey from the Pit of Hades to the Garden of Eden. But here in Eden it was colder than at home, and the biting wind was nipping at my face and neck, even through the gloves on my hands. I saw my first groves of lemons, limes and oranges, though I had seen some straggly trees before and I had eaten their fruit. The early Spaniards had also planted date palms, which had to have been a hundred years old and now towered high, with their new leaf-branches waving in the upper air and the old dried fronds protecting the trunks of the trees as if cloaking them with hanging shields. The huge aromatic pepper trees carried all their leaves even in the cold winter, but the clusters of small corns were very green with occasional wrinkled black corns missed from an earlier harvest.

I arrived tired in the late evening, and as if I'd been a weary traveler in the days of the Californios, the padres invited me to their renowned supper. The Butterfield Stage Line used the western rooms of the convento, or priests' quarters; the dining room was next to the stage line, and the kitchen was immediately adjacent. Several rooms of the second floor were for weary guests, who ascended by an adobe stairway leading off the kitchen. A padre told me the convento was the longest adobe building in California, 243 feet long and 50 feet wide. The16 foot-high portico was formed by a colonnade of 21 arches. It was not attached to the church, but was separate and facing El Camino Real, The King's Highway.

The food was plentiful and tasty, with spices not found at our Mission San Gabriel, not even in the best houses and hotels of Los Angeles. I ate more cooked beef than I had ever eaten in one meal, with tortillas and tea. Not only was there a large dish of stewed frijoles, there was a salad of fresh ripe tomatoes sprinkled with olive oil and vinegar and seasoned with several spices and salts. And this in the middle of a freezing winter!

I couldn't understand this. "Padre, how can you have fresh tomatoes in the cold of winter?" I asked. "I can feel snow in the air, and yet it is summer in your kitchen!"

Padre Juan answered proudly. "We dig up our tomato plants at the end of the season and hang the vines, with their roots still in clumps of soil, upside down in the cellars," Padre Juan answered proudly. "The tomatoes are watered through their soil and roots and slowly ripen when placed next to apples. This is a process that occurs even when it is freezing outside."

After dinner, Padre Juan continued talking about their gardens. "Come with me for a short walk to our orangerie. This is our French word for orange grove. Would you enjoy an orange for dessert?"

"I sure would," I said wishing I knew what dessert meant.

He then gave me a whole orange; he even allowed me to pick it from the tree!

"Mr. King, would you now enjoy a postprandial brandy from our vineyard? It's as good as any made in Mexico. Come, join us by the fireplace."

Again I didn't know what a postprandial brandy was, but if it was as good as the meal and orange, whatever it was would be enjoyable. Speaking as elegantly as I could, I replied, "Certainly, Padre. I would be pleased to join you and your friends."

What an end to this day which had begun with sneaking off by the light of the setting moon and now ended in front of a real fireplace with an oaken mantel, sitting in a chair and not on the floor or a bench. And we were sipping brandy from an imported, long-stemmed Italian glass! It was my first taste of fine cognac, as he named it, and the first time I had drunk from such an elegant glass. I decided that this was the manner of life I desired. But the drink also loosened my thoughts and my tongue.

Father Juan, a man about two decades older than me, spoke excellent English. He inquired, "Why is such a young man as yourself riding away from home in the dead of winter? You have committed no offense, I pray. I see you have a holster on your left side. Praise God there is no weapon in it."

Instinctively I grasped for the shoulder holster, and then remembered I had left the Dragoon in its envelope on the saddle in the barn. "No, Padre. I seek to kill a man for killing my father, Sheriff Samuel King. Pa was bushwhacked by Micajah Johnson, who shot him in the back three days ago. Micajah left El Diablo ridin the skin off'en his horse for The Windy Pass, and I'm goin'a git him."

"My son, retribution is only for God on the Day of Redemption. Retribution is not in man's domain. We cannot usurp that which is His alone to determine. You will be damned from that day on. I pray of you to forgive Micajah in your heart, that you may enjoy your life in a Godly way and sleep well without revisiting your victim nightly. Let Micajah answer to God, as he will."

"Father, I seek revenge and to uphold the honor of my family. For what is done to one is done to all. An eye for an eye, a tooth for a tooth, just as the Bible says. My father died alone in a dusty street. Now I will kill Johnson in the dust and dirt."

"Son, it is already winter. Frost is on the earth in the morning. I feel snow in the air, and in the mountains, the trails will be treacherous. The wind is building, bringing wet air from the west, and the temperature is falling. If the westerly wind blows over these mountains, there could be a major storm and you will not survive. There is no camp between here and the Tehachapi. If you are able to get there, you will be entering Micajah's territory, as he must have fled to Tehachapi for a reason. You may not find any friends there, perhaps only enemies. How do you know he was riding there? Perhaps he left for San Francisco. He certainly was not seen here, not even on the Butterfield Stage."

I was so angry at what the padre was saying that I didn't hear most of it.

"Son, think about this overnight. I'll be pleased if you would join me for an early breakfast."

"Thank you, Padre. I'll be pleased to join you for breakfast, as I must get an early start."

"If you don't reconsider, it may be the last breakfast you'll ever eat. I would never allow anyone from our mission to undertake a journey through these mountains in the middle of January, and never with a storm arriving out of the west."

"Padre, I know I'll catch him, and Pa's gun will kill him. I've ridden out many a Texas plains storm, and I can do it in these mountains too."

"Don't anger your God! Remember, my son, those who dug up the floors of this mission, and searched for the rumored gold, found no gold but only injury at the hands of others, and dishonor from the church and the true God.

"And what makes you, a very young man, believe you can survive a gunfight against a professional? Please reconsider this ill-advised act. I'll see you in the morn. God bless you."

"Padre, I thank you for your thoughts and best wishes. But I, too, am a professional, and I have God and the law on my side. I will survive and avenge my father."

Although tired, I did not sleep well. What was it about this weather that was so dangerous? I had survived the blizzards of the Texas plains, where there were no hills to protect and shelter the traveler, although in summer we built lean-tos and huts for the coming winter storms and stocked them with firewood and wraps.

My thoughts of the chase and pending gunfight kept me awake most of the night. The harsh screams of the mission's peacocks startled me into wakefulness whenever I began to sleep. I was now a believer that a peacock makes an excellent watchdog for they shrieked whenever a leaf stirred in the garden that night, much less an intruder. I would suggest to Padre Juan in the morning that he add these colorful, long plumed-chickens to his evening meals; his guests would not only eat more but also sleep better.

My thoughts returned to my family and my murdered father. Johnson had destroyed all I held dear to me. I would make him pay. My life would never be the same. No longer could we sit at night by our pot-bellied stove, Frank, Sam and me, passing a cheroot from one to another, talking about our day's work, planning the next day's chores, while waiting for our hard-working father to return to a late supper. I remember one of our last talks, when we wondered about the new Mexican vice, that of small narrow cigars wrapped in paper, not good tobacco leaf; -cigarettes they were called. Probably any tobacco in them was scraped from the cutting room floors. I knew that Ma would never give up her beloved corncob pipe for them as she joined us after her work was done.

In the early morning the fathers gave me a hearty Mexican breakfast, an olla podrida with frijoles, shortcake and tea. It is no wonder that even the younger padres were rotund. They had been up for hours, and their converted Indian slaves, or neophytes, were already working in the fields when I set off in the early dawn. What a pleasant life if I could only settle down on a ranch like this. But it had already been too late for us to do so when we arrived in 1852. Was it, even now, too late for the padres and the Californios as well?

The early morning sun brightened the south-facing convento and created shadows that highlighted features, unseen in the evening darkness. Some of the arches were revealed as only remnants of ruins; most arches showed extensive weathering, with destruction of the covering plaster and whitewash. The ground-floor rooms were almost fully destroyed, with the exception of those used as an office by the Butterfield Stage, the small makeshift inn where we had dined so elegantly last night, and the kitchen. The cellar where the tomato vines hung upside down was actually a ground-floor room, the former wine cellar of the mission. There were gaping holes in the adobe floors where scavengers had dug for the padres' gold after the local discovery in 1842, following the myth that the mission padres had buried their treasures beneath their floors.

How different the mission must have appeared when Colonel Fremont occupied the convento as his headquarters during the Mexican War in 1846. Ma's lessons had taught me that Governor Pio Pico had leased the mission to his brother, General Andreas Pico, who later sold it and pocketed the monies himself. Now, by daylight, I could see that even the tiles of the roof had been taken by local settlers for their own hovels and only a few second-floor rooms were habitable, to be used by the occasional traveler.

The neophytes were few in number, and chiefly women with small children. There were no priests to be seen; I recalled again what Ma had taught us: after a long war, New Spain had gained independence from Spain in 1821, renamed itself Mexico and, in 1834, secularized most of the missions after Spain discontinued supporting them financially. Mexico had then started giving large grants of former mission land to its citizens, in order to prevent the land from falling under control of the English and Russians.

I wondered if Padre Juan had been appointed to be in charge of the mission, or if he and the others were merely squatters, eking out a living while performing God's duties. From what I observed, the San Fernando Mission could not have sent men to the Amargosa Desert to rescue the Manley Party. In terms of numbers and worldly goods, the mission residents were barely survivors themselves and must have exhausted their carefully husbanded foods upon my two meals. But they had welcomed a weary traveler in the grand old Californio manner.

Soon we rode out of the flat-lands and Star slowly climbed an old Indian path through the switchbacks, north up San Francisquito Canyon. Winter was here, and it was cold and damp when we reached the mile-high summit. Even at noon there was ice in the shaded crevices of the trail, and when small muddy potholes lay in the shadows, they were glazed with patterns of thin cracked ice. I could not set Star to trotting, as it was too slippery and dangerous. Sometimes the narrow, rocky path was only slippery shale that sloped down to the cliff side where the canyon fell for hundreds of feet. Star's hoofs would slip and slide on the loose scree, and I held my breath so often my heart was pounding continuously. I determined it was safer to dismount and walk. A slip here would disable and probably even kill us; for once over the edge there was only one stop during the fall…the last one.

The dull lowering pewter-clad clouds were harmonious with the mountains and my feelings-that of a coming storm and increasing danger. Would my destruction come from the weather, or was Johnson lying in wait?

"Slow down Star. That's it. Steady boy. I got to dismount.

"Hold on now. I'm just taking this little tie down off the horn."

The horse pistol envelope opened easy. The Dragoon slipped into my shoulder harness without difficulty. The hours spent in reworking the harness were well worth the time. I tightened the tie down over the butt of the Dragoon. I would be totally lost if the big pistol fell over the canyon edge as my little hide out in my right jacket pocket would be useless in a shootout. I felt better after this, more protected from Johnson, for I could fight back. But the following storm continued to steadily build in depth and intensity. Would I survive? Could I survive? Were the heavens foretelling my stormy future?

Higher up, the path widened to almost a horse trail, and I remounted and increased Star's pace. There were still narrow shelves of strongly sloping and slippery bare rock, falling off the side of the mountain for hundreds of feet. Here, I dismounted and led Star. But when riding, sometimes my left shoulder was already brushing the perpendicular up-slope wall and there was no room to dismount. I was lucky just to remain in my saddle. Even the Indians must have trod carefully at these places.

As I climbed higher through the clouds, the sun glared through patches in the foggy mist. I saw small green side valleys above the trail leading into the canyon, with patches of old snow on the northern, shady slopes. The crusted surface of the snow with its diamond like crystals reflected the slanting rays of sun. A few cattle were grazing on the verdant green, and there were small herds of deer. Fawning had not yet begun and the does were full bellied. Small springs and rivulets appeared in almost every valley although there was seldom a flow of water across the trail. A hunter could live well here.

After passing Elizabeth Lake, I took the path towards Stockton turning east to Willow Springs. The sun was low behind my shoulder and had no heat in it. I kept to the left side of the now broad but untraveled trail, searching for a protected camping spot from the coming storm. Despite it being so cold that water froze in sheets over shadowed trickles of water, the threatening storm had not yet arrived in the mountains surrounding the high desert.

In the late afternoon, the darkening sky turned leaden in color and weight. It felt as if it would sink and crush me if I could not find shelter immediately. Walnut-sized ice balls of hail scattered like grapeshot across the plain and I could see them bouncing off the closer hills. The wet clouds from the ocean must be confronting the cold northern winds. This storm was truly stronger than the storms of the Texas plains.

Long flashes of lightening lit the hills behind me, strong enough to cast my shadow forward. These were followed by five-minute tattoos of thunder with intrusive cracking of giant whips as other bolts struck the earth close to us. Fortunately Star was too tired to respond to commands other than mine, although he jumped when hit by the large balls of hail. Icy flakes continually struck us-they certainly did not fall gently as snow upon us. When I saw a small rock outcropping with a steep western side running north and south, I knew I had found protection from the westerly storm. I dismounted and led Star up the draw until we were protected from the howling wind blowing through the main canyon.

I short-tied Star to a bush on the western side of the outcropping, and stomped down a small circle of brush for a campsite, leaving scrub and bushes around us for protection from low, wind driven snow. I foraged for grass and small branches of green sage, and used them to dry and curry Star's winter hair. I reversed his saddle blankets, so the dry sides were against his hide and cinched them moderately tight so they wouldn't slip. I added some of the grass to his feed, to bulk up his corn and oats.

After seeing to Star, I built a small fire pit. Larger river stones were placed against the west side of the draw in a semicircle, five to six boulders high against the bank, so the heat would be reflected back towards us. The fire pit was a small oval depression, about a foot deep, lined with flat rocks, some built up over the edge and reaching out so my pot would balance level. The wind was deflected by the thick brush to the apex of my open chimney, drawing towards the rear and upwards. I collected dried brush stems and branches, as well as any wood I could find. Some larger branches had floated down the small arroyo during previous storms and I dragged them close to the fire pit. I saved the dry inner shavings from the branches as I cut and whittled them into smaller sticks for the fire, my body protecting them from the falling snow. After leaning them together, tee-pee fashion, I struck my Lucifer, cupping it with my gloved hands. I was pleased to smell the sulfur from its lighting surface, and to see it catch fire. I was even happier to see the shavings catch fire the first time. Building with ever-larger branches, my small fire was soon burning strongly despite the falling, wet snow; my body provided shelter from the snow at the beginning. Branches stacked around the rim of the fire pit protected the fire from sudden gusts of wind and snow, and dried the branches for burning later. Little smoke developed and even that could not be seen through the brush when I stepped back a few feet. If Micajah were watching for me, he would have a hard time spotting my campsite.

But where was Micajah? I had not seen traces of his trail. Had he slipped over the edge and fallen to his death? Was the padre right? Did he go to Frisco despite naming the Tehachapis? Or was he so far ahead I would never find him? He could not have traveled faster than I, nor could he have traveled longer, for I rode from the false dawn until darkness upon a strong horse. I must have gained half-a-day in the chase. Or was he waiting to ambush me from a favorable hidie-hole today?

Worries aside, I could now heat my supper, melt snow for drinking, and later, bank the fire for warming us somewhat throughout the freezing night. There was a dampish cold seeping down from the surrounding hills and the heavy, cold, wet fog streamed down our draw as if it were water flowing into a catchment area. Star and I needed this protective hillside even if the full storm did not reach us.

I watered Star again and adjusted the ground cover over his neck and back, trying to make a small hood over his head. I cinched the cover loosely around his neck and tail, as well as around his girth. Finally, I tied him to a low bush just within range of the heat from the fire, close to the side of the arroyo and upwind, so his body would provide some protection for me. After all, his kind had survived stormy weather for thousands of years.

I cut more brush to provide a layer of insulation for my bedroll, I spread grass and small twigs on the wet ground for protection from the ice cold, wet earth and the driven snow, then leafy branches went on top of the cut ground growth. More brush was piled on to provide even more ground insulation for my bedroll. I rolled out my bottom tarp beyond where my head would be, moved my saddle to the head end, and folded the edge of the tarp back over my saddle. Short stems of brush lifted the end of the tarp up and over my head and face, providing a 6-inch-high protective hood. I carefully folded my blankets in alternate layers, both top and bottom, really doubling their thickness.

I slept only fitfully, with a cold body and disturbing dreams. When I awoke, it was still dark. My head had slipped off the seat of the saddle, but my face was completely underneath the top flap of the hood. Small, hoary, lacey icicles hung down the edge of the tarp over my nose where the moisture in my breath had frozen. I imperceptibly changed my position and peeked out, searching for a possible attacker. Snowflakes drifted down in front of my face, but I saw no one. Before leaving the protection of my bedroll, I reached down inside where my boots were, slowly pulling them on over my socks. Because my body heat had radiated through my bedding and into the snow topping, there was a thin crust of ice around me that crackled as I moved under the ground cover. I stood up, shaking, and brushed about 2 inches of snow off my driver's duster. Then I reached between my bedding, got out my Dragoon and rifle and checked their loads. To my relief, I found them dry.

I had left both water skins wrapped into my bedroll, and despite my body heat, they were frozen solid. It was the last time I would do that! The sparse wood I had collected had been dampened by the mist and light snowfall, but only on their top layers; I could still burn them for heating coffee. I looked into the clear sky; it was apparent that the storm had blown by overnight, although it had left behind five inches of fresh snow.

I broke camp early. As I gazed back from a 20-foot distance, I could see no sign of where I had spent the night. Overhead branches had not heated and my camp location was not disclosed by the absence of snow or the presence of icicles on branches, indicating that the snow had melted and then refrozen while dripping.

On the high valley desert floor, the sun shone upon a glistening plain of snow, smooth except for the irregularities of the ground and a few bushes. Small tracks made by desert rodents, a few rabbits from the foothills, and one coyote trailing after its wanted meal disclosed the peacefulness for man but the terror of daily living for others. Star made the only large prints in the winter wilderness. The cold, dry, high desert winds were in control. Pa's Dragoon in my shoulder holster reminded me of him and comforted me.

For the next two days I rode hard and fast along the northern foothills of the Tehachapi Mountains. The weather warmed and the snow on the ground disappeared. Finally, I found an Indian trail leading north to the mountain's summit. But where was Micajah? I had seen no trail signs of him. Had he disappeared? Was he so far in front of me that I couldn't catch him? How could that be? I had ridden fast and certainly gained on him, even though the trail was new to me. Both Star and I were exhausted, but I would not quit until I caught him. I must catch him, and soon.

The trail twisted and turned as it climbed the Windy Pass, as Tehachapi is known. Soon I could see many prints of horse hooves, both shod and unclad. Hanging valleys, usually with spumy waterfalls blown by the constant wind, were on both sides of the trail. I was fortunate to possess a warm, airtight oilskin duster, as the cold spray from the falls often blew over me. My hat blew off once, and I had to put spurs to Star in chasing it across the valley floor. I then tightened the chin-strap so it would not happen again. The oaks on the hills grew twisted, bent to the east, obeying the powerful commands of the strong winds that always blew out of the west. My kerchief blew in the same direction, but it was tied gently around my neck and did not fly away. Ant there was no wind strong enough to blow my 4 ½-pound Dragoon away!

Gradually, the narrow Windy Pass opened into a plain with small valleys of grasses and gushing springs spilling down. Herds of deer and antelope thrived here, and were not frightened at seeing me a mile away. I rode past peaceful and friendly tribes of Indians who inhabited this verdant area. Some whites lived in the area too. They had made bush houses by throwing canvas over large brushes, tying the billowing edges down close to the roots so their home walls wouldn't blow away.

In the late afternoon, I saw a distant stick-and-sod house abutting a hillock. There was one door in the front but no windows. The structure was very narrow, only two dobe bricks in width, butting into the knoll in the back. The back part of the sod building must have been dug into the steep hillside or else it was built in front of a cave. I rode silently toward it and soon identified it as a saloon because there were four horses at the hitching post out front.

One hard-ridden horse, gaunt and exhausted, was quivering all over. Dirty white lather was dried around its muzzle, and its hide was caked white with salts from sweat. The saddle was covered with small clumps of dirt thrown up by hoofs and appeared to be falling apart from lack of care. This horse must belong to Micajah, for its usage and lack of care described a man whose only goal was running away. Only a man on the run would treat his mount this way.

As I approached the saloon from the south, Star and I threw a long shadow in front of us. I veered 30 feet to the west of the path so our shadow would not alert the drinkers to our approach. I slowly dismounted, ground looped Star, and hoped the horses would not neigh to one another. Hopefully the murdering bushwhacker was inside! I wanted to surprise the drinkers into giving up Micajah so I could deal with him alone.

I walked slowly and silently toward the sod house. Then I stopped, jolted as if hit by lightning! I was not armed! I had forgotten to transfer my Pa's gun to my shoulder holster! It was still in its envelope, tier to the pommel of my saddle. Micajah could kill me and I could do nothing! I hurried back to Star, untied the envelope of the holster, slipped the thong off the hammer, checked the loads in the chambers, and thrust the Dragoon into my shoulder holster on my left side.

Then I injuned up to the sod house. I got so close I could hear loud, angry voices, although I could not understand the individual words or sentences that bellowed out through the open door. Finally, when I stood close to the entrance, I could hear them bragging about robberies and gunfights. Then a strident, high voice began boasting about killing Dad in a shoot-out on Main Street of the Monte.

"I killed that old coot out of Georgia," the voice said. "He was standing there, sucking air in the middle of Main Street, right in front of me when I called him down. I could see his eyes rolling and looking around, trying to find a place to hide. But there was nowhere to hide. He begged me not to shoot him: 'I got a whelp of kids at home. Leave me be. I won't never bother you, never see you no more. Just let me go.'

"Then he snaked his hand down his pants, drawin his hawg leg, bringing it up the best he could, for he was shaking all over. I drew and shot him three times right in his heart. I walked over and saw he was dead. Everyone had seen him draw first and I wasn't even charged."

Doing my best not to strangle on my anger and tears, I walked backward twenty feet into the sun that was shining directly into the open doorway. Still no one had seen me. I yelled with as much authority as my young voice could give me: "Johnson, come out of there! I'll fight you man to man. This time you can't shoot me in the back as you did Dad.

You're a dirty yellow bushwhacking coward! And a liar, too!"

All was silent. Then slowly, four shadowy faces peered out of the darkness of the hut into the blurring sun. "He ain't nothing but a kid!" exclaimed one deep sepulcher voice.

Further silence. Then two dissolute men stepped out and away from the hut with their hands at shoulder height, squinting into the sun and separating from one another as they walked away.

"Which one of you is Johnson?" I yelled. "He's the only one I want. You others can walk away. But I'm gonna get em!"

I strode two steps toward the two in the open.

"Don't shoot! Don't shoot," one of the men shouted. "You got no argument with me. I don't even know this here Johnson!"

"Neither do I," the second man cried out. "I just stopped in for a drink!"

"You two!" I said to them. "Keep your hands up and walk away! Drop your gun belts and keep on walking if you want'a live!"

I turned towards the saloon and stepped to the southwest side. I would not be seen clearly from the inside as now, the sun was shining from directly behind me.

My thoughts and all my senses were only upon Johnson. I could not see him or hear him. Was he going to shot me from the darkness as he had Pa? To kill me, to leave me to die in the dusty trail?

I must be brave as if expecting him to come out and stand like a man. To make my will overpower him and to perform as I wished.

"Come out Johnson, prepare to meet your Maker, for I am here!" I yelled. "You're a cowardly bushwhacker and you shot my Pa in the back. He had no chance, but I'm a givin you one!"

A man with a tired face, jowls sunk down on his jaw bones, shuffled out of the darkness into the afternoon sun, and just stood there. He was unshaven and unwashed, with a week's mud spattered on his head and clothes. His shoulders and arms carried the muscles of his blacksmithing, and his big, meaty hands confirmed years of hard work, but his skin had slackened and was no longer firm. He didn't appear to be a young cowboy. Was this really Johnson?

I could see nothing in the world, only Johnson. His long, dirty reddish-blonde hair was unkempt. He wore a sweaty, dirty kerchief around his neck, his shirt was dirty even for an extended trail, and he was missing the top two buttons. He must have dry-camped all the way, and must have been so fearful of me that he had slept only fitfully. Johnson's chest moved rapidly up and down, and his breath whistled as it blew out. I could hear it plainly, as well as the slight wind blowing over my shoulder and past my ear, the rustling of our clothes, the creak of our leather holsters and gun belts as I stepped forward, the sound of my boots hitting the dust and dirt of the ground, jangling of my California spurs.

My left side was crabbed slightly toward him, my body hiding the slow movement of my lowered right arm bending from the elbow upward toward my waist. I began sweating under my hat brim. My breathing became rapid and my fingers tingled. I could see Johnson's nervousness, with his sweaty brow, the holding of his indrawn breath, and the jerky involuntary movements of his hands as if he were attempting to draw his gun several times a second.

Suddenly, a sweat bee landed on my right hand. Without thinking, I jerked my hand away and batted it down.

"Watch out, he's throwing down!" yelled the sepulcher voice out of the darkness of the bar.

Johnson began drawing his gun. He was drawing first and, as with Pa, it was not going to be a fair fight!

I lifted my right arm and began to draw my Dragoon across my body, continuing to stride forward.

I couldn't draw the gun out of its holster! It had caught on my coat! I used my left hand to pull my coat back, and then the Dragoon finally came clear. However, my stride was broken and I lost my balance. Johnson fired but missed, perhaps because I was stumbling. Finally, I regained my balance. I extended and planted my right foot, and began to swing the pistol forward and down. Johnson fired again, but I felt nothing. He fired again. My Dragoon now was horizontal and I aimed carefully at Johnson. My right arm was extended, with the revolver pointed like a finger toward him. Gently, my right index finger squeezed closed. The cartridge exploded, the big gun kicked and roared, and a cloud of smoke billowed forward. I heard a heavy thump as the big slug hit firm flesh.

Johnson was slammed so hard by the ball that he straightened up. I brought the gun down and squeezed the trigger again and again; he was beaten backwards, blown over by the heavy shots. Johnson hit the dirt and, a few seconds later, he began that rhythmic dance of death: the heels digging in the dust with his toes two stepping in the air, his bent arms boxing an unknown assailant, all to the silent tune of the danse macabre. When he finally stopped moving, he was grinning in the rictus of death and the front of his pants showed dark and wet, and he began to stink.

Now, I fixed my eyes solely upon the second figure; who appeared lost as he stumbled out of the saloon with his hands in the air. "Don't shoot, compadre!" he said. "I don't know that Johnson! He came riding in this noon and had a few drinks. That's all!"

"Drop your gun belt to the ground now!"

"Yes, sir. There, it's on the ground now."

"I want you and your two friends back in the saloon. Pronto. Now! Without your shootin' irons," I said. "I'll sit back a ways with my rifle to be sure you stay put. Just leave Johnson there in the dirt. That's where he's going anyway. If there's any gold in his pockets, use it to bury him."

Another question occurred to me. "Where is the Alcade? I want to report this attempt upon my life. You all saw Johnson draw and shoot first."

The man with the sepulcher voice responded. "He lives in that adobe house back where the trail divides, going toward the stream. He'll be there if not huntin' dinner."

After the three men disappeared into the saloon, I walked backward to Star, always watching the open door. I grabbed Star's reins, mounted, and backed him up, still keeping a close watch on the dark opening of the bar. I retreated about a hundred yards down the trail, stopped, and waited.

A long piece of iron slowly poked through the doorway, followed by a face that peered over the rifle. I immediately put a rifle bullet into the crosspiece of the door frame, just above the shooter's head. He jerked back inside so fast that he lost his grip and the rifle fell to the ground. I didn't want to kill him, just keep him and the other two inside so they could not shoot me. Once I had demonstrated that I meant what I said, I waited a minute and then quietly rode out of the valley, headin' home.

I looked up to the heavens above me. I had never seen the sky bluer, the clouds whiter, the setting sun so red and the clouds upon which it rested so crimson and gold. I had never been able to see so far or so clear. I smelled the fresh breezes as they rolled over the grasses and brush, the slight acrid smell of sage, and the cloying sweet aroma of anis. My nasal passages absorbed sweet water vapor as I approached streams. I could smell waterfalls from a distance. I felt the cold of the vapor from the snow packs; it almost caused a sharp pain as it entered my lungs. I had never been so alive, and I knew I could fly away into the skies. I was Atlas and I carried the earth on my shoulders. There was no pain in me.


Soon, everything changed. I slowly rode down the mountain, letting Star find the trail home. Exhaustion settled over my mind and body. I couldn't think or plan. I found it difficult to raise my head and look forward. My eyes looked only upon the ground immediately in front of Star. My vision blurred. The world dimmed and then darkened, although it was only early evening and I knew I was riding into the setting sun. The bushes were indistinct, their outlines blurred and doubled. My entire body shook for minutes at a time and then I became limp, just sitting on Star as he ambled onward. My body turned to fluid and I had to dismount and relieve myself so as not to soil my clothes. I could ride no further, so I made a cold camp without eating, caring only for Star, then rolling out my bedroll.

I was not fated to die as a young man, for I was good, not bad. As I stood there with those shots of death flying by, God was showing me my future. I would be a man of stature, just as I was a man of family. Others might die, but I would not. I would prevail and my line would not die out!

Yet, I have known good men to die. My father was one, dying alone on a dusty street, performing his duty to the community. Where were his promised threescore and ten? Was death just haphazard? How is a man selected? How did God reconcile Johnson shooting at me and missing, then my shooting at him and striking him dead as if I were an avenging biblical God? Or was I, the earthly actor, performing His wishes?

What good was all of this? How did it help my father, who was lost forever?

Did Johnson have a woman and children? What was the young Padre Juan really trying to tell me? Would it have been different if I had been a sheriff leading a posse after Johnson? If our community of men had declared Johnson a killer, would I have been sanctified to kill him? Would God then have been appeased?

I realized I was but a youth, lacking experience in many things except how to survive life. I had not feared death. I had known I would successfully avenge my father. I hadn't even considered that my quest might fail; that I might be the one to fall, that I might die.

If I were lucky, perhaps I could be as good a person as my father. Perhaps it was enough that I had learned to stay alive. Or was I an angeli rebelli? After all, God's original angels were performing works of the Devil. Why hadn't I felt this way after killing murdering Indians or banditos?

Why do I have these repetitious dreams after so many years?

When I returned to the Pueblo, I learned that Micajah Johnson was not a young cowboy, but an old man of 55 years who had traveled in a wagon train from Ohio with family. His wife and one baby girl had died crossing the plains. He continued on to the Monte with five young daughters. What did I do to them? And what would happen to them now? How would they survive?

I cried then. Some nights, I still do.

# Laura, Angel of Los Angeles

It was a wonderful, warm spring day with songbirds warbling and twitting and occasional bunnies hopping across the trail as they playfully chased one another. But now it was 1861, although my thoughts involuntarily kept returning to that same horse trail which I had ridden in the spring of 1856. Perhaps it was the goal of the journey was driving my memories back five years to 1856- the Rancho Santa Ana del Chino. This year, I had been invited again to the Rancho Santa Ana del Chino. The trail from Los Angeles remained 40 miles and when a good horse was ridden on a light canter, one could still arrive before noon with an early morning departure. And on this beautiful morning, I had again started early as I had done five years ago. The repetitious rhythm of the 3 beat canter lulled my thoughts to 1856, that year after my father had been murdered, and to my initial invitation to the Hacienda…

Despite my father's murder last year, my senses overwhelmed me into accepting and silently acknowledging it was a wonderful spring day! Perhaps it was the circumstances of the purpose of my trip as much as the greening of the fields and the warmth of the sun. I was invited to the Rancho Santa Ana del Chino! The Rancho was a significant portion of the huge land grant deeded to Antonio Maria Lugo by Carlos the Third, King of Spain, and which had descended by marriage dowry to Isaac Williams, that old trapper who thereafter, suddenly had developed a great amount of wisdom and political knowledge. Williams was given the honorific of Don Julian soon after his receipt of the dowry. It was said that he kept a large vase of golden doubloons by his doorway, and everyone who left his home could take as many as needed. No word was ever mentioned regarding repayment.

I invited Sam and Francis to go with me, but they declined because of work on their ranches. I suspected they declined because they would feel uncomfortable in the political atmosphere of the Rancho but since I had avenged our father's death last year, I had become a noted man in Los Angeles, one marked for destiny with a bright future.

Star and I gradually trotted up to an exquisitely dressed fellow traveler on the trail to the valley.

"Hello there friend," I cried out. "Are you also visiting Colonel Williams?"

I said this to show I was non-threatening, and frankly, to impress the stranger as to whom I was visiting. "My name is Andrew Jackson King and I work for the Sheriff of Los Angeles and also as an assistant to the First County Clerk for San Bernardino County."

I could swear his initial facial response was of surprise, then immediately one showing dismay, and finally, a furtive response of secretiveness as if he had been dealt an unusual hand when playing cards.

"I'm pleased to meet you. I, too, am visiting the Colonel and his family at the Rancho Chino. I'm Robert S. Carlisle, friend of the family. Shall we ride together? It's still a ways to go."

"Yes, Mr. Carlisle. Thank you. Our journey will go more comfortably when shared by two." And it did.

Mr. Carlisle was educated, and he too, was of the Southern persuasion. Just speaking with him enhanced my vocabulary and educated me as to the better grammar of an honorable Southern gentleman. If he were an example of Col. Williams and his friends, I must be reticent in my speech, for it would excluded me from their society if I would speak unguardedly and demonstrate my lack of education. Attendance at a one room grammar school in Helena, Arkansas is not the finest recommendation. Even on our ride to Rancho Chino, I must be careful as to what I said, and especially how I said it.

Why did Carlisle know my name and why was he on guard against me? What was wrong here? The only bit of notoriety I achieved in Los Angeles was avenging my Pa's murder by shooting Micajah Johnson a year ago January. But that was no reason for this gentleman, carrying two guns on his hip, to abhor my action or even to mention it. Any son from the South would have responded as I had. Carlisle cast many a glance at the horse pistol envelope attached to the pommel of my saddle and then up to both sides of my buttoned coat. I knew he could not see the lines of the empty holster underneath the left side, but what was the purpose of this close examination? Did he want to know if I ever carried my gun on my person?

"There are several King families in our Los Angeles area now. Are you perhaps related to the late Samuel King, Sheriff out of Dahlonega, Georgia?"

At last, it was out. But it imparted little knowledge to me other than he was aware of Pa. "Yes, Sir," I responded. "He was my father."

"I was sorry to hear of his death. He was a good man. Is it not true that another member of his family killed Johnson, the man who shot him?"

"Yes, Sir. That is correct." Why is he asking this? How could he recall this so accurately, even the name of Pa's murderer, when sudden deaths occurred daily in Los Angeles? Why was this personally important to him? If he knew about Pa's murder, he must certainly know that I was the avenger. I must answer fully and immediately. I did not wish to gull him but neither did I wish to alert him as to my increasing mistrust.

"In fact, Sir, I was fortunate to be the son who performed that deed himself."

"You were correct in your handling of the matter. Before you shot Johnson, did you speak with him at all? Did he say anything to you about a reason for bushwhacking your father?"

Why was Carlisle so interested in the possible passage of information from Johnson to me? What reason was he talking about? Why was it of concern to him? Was Carlisle involved in my father's murder?

"No, Sir. Johnson said very little. He was so scared he could hardly speak. Why?" There, I hope that satisfies him although it does not actually deny passage of information.

"Oh, nothing. I can't even remember if I ever met him." And then we rode silently on. I didn't believe his last statement but didn't know how to continue our talk.

"There! Ahead of us is the Hacienda Santa Ana del Chino. We can't see because of the rising sun, but it lies in the heart of a fertile valley facing eastwards! The Colonel has repaired it since the traitorous attack by the Californios and then the Americans back in September of 1846. It has again become the largest and best private home in California. And it belongs to a true patriot, despite what many jealous men say."

Carlisle's words failed to fully describe the beauty of the house and the immediate gardens but they disclosed his liking for the Colonel, or at least for his possessions. We were riding out of the hills and the valley lay beneath us. The house was in the shape of a square, with each side about 250 feet long. The thick walls were made of adobe and the roof was sealed with brea, which was reflecting the silvery light of the sun's rays off the flat roof. A part of the roof was two floors high, almost unknown for a hacienda in this county.

Servants must have been watching for arriving guests. When we reached the entry of the house, one immediately assisted us in dismounting, then led our horses to one of the adjacent farm buildings. Another opened the Judas door, a single frame of the huge double door at the entrance, and bowed as we entered. The first object I noted was the bowl filled with doubloons for the departing guest with such a need. The famous vase did exist!

We noted large religious shrines on both sides of the entry hall as we walked into the square patio, an open courtyard with a slowly moving stream of water in a zanja pouring into the basin of a fountain. The heat of the sun had caused some of the brea to soften and run down the side of the walls in dark black spidery lines. We knew we had penetrated too far as we were now in the private family area of the home. We retreated back down the hallway and found the parlor with its arched doorway partially obscured by a Chinese screen.

After we had walked into the private area of the house, I immediately knew that house was unfamiliar to Carlisle despite his earlier declaration. I was determined to be even more circumspect to all here, especially Carlisle who by now, did not ring true.

We knocked gently on the screen and entered the parlor. I immediately forgot all my thoughts and planning for this important meeting. I could see only this vivacious, intelligent, brown haired, brown eyed girl who was just entering young womanhood. I was later informed she was only fifteen but already had experiences of a lifetime. .

I had seen her at San Gabriel for at least a year, but only now, in this unexpected personal encounter did I recognize how special she was. Miss Laura Evertsen-who arrived in Los Angeles when she was only seven years old back in the fall of '49. Her family had endured a hard nine month journey by ox train out of San Antonio, Texas. Indians had attacked them on the trail and killed or driven off all the oxen, horses, and other livestock. The Evertsen party remained stranded in the wilderness for months until other California bound travelers came by, and assisted them on their way to San Gabriel.

And then, when they finally arrived in San Gabriel, the Evertsens discovered that their promised abode did not exist, and they were forced to travel further to Los Angeles and stay there until they built their home, *The Locust*, by the mission.

Even now, I could well visualize her as a seven year old girl loading the rifles and pistols with powder and shot, then passing the guns to her elders for firing, or even aiming and pulling the trigger herself against the marauding savages.

Despite her brown eyes and brown hair, there was no question about her Viking ancestry, standing straight and tall against the world. What a woman! I wish I could have been there to help. I guess I fell in love that day, for the first and only time.

I had already heard her family was prominent in New York and although I had never met him, personally knew of her powerful father who took the first U.S. Census of Los Angeles in 1850 as the *District Assistant to the Census Marshall of California* and was now the elected alcalde of San Gabriel.

And today, I would meet her socially, no more to stand in the distance and to see a little girl pass, as suddenly she was a young woman, the age of my mother when she married Pa. And I was now 20, a man standing tall in my own right.

Unexpectedly, Colonel Williams was by my side and speaking. I had paid no attention to any of the crowd, only the vision of Laura. I was even unaware of what his first words were. This alert man must have noted my scrutiny of Laura and the adulation in my eyes. He placed his hand on my arm as he walked me across the parlor. He probably could feel the tenseness in my muscles as we approached her.

"Miss Evertsen, I would like to present to you, an up and coming young man in our community, a man who has already proven his strength. Mr. Andrew Jackson King.

"AJ, this is Miss Laura Evertsen, one of the brightest stars in our firmament. We, in our new City of the Angels, hold her as one of our dearest as well." After these accolades, the great man retired to his family and friends, leaving us alone. I continued to neglect the remainder of the guests, and even forgot about the foreboding presence of Carlisle.

"Miss Evertsen, I have admired you from a distance. It is now my opportunity to meet you. Please address me as AJ. My friends do, and truly, I would like to have you as a friend and enjoy your friendship."

"I shall be pleased to call you AJ, as I and everyone in town already do. Please address me as Laura for we have heard so much about you, I already acknowledge you as a friend."

My heart jumped. I could feel it losing a beat, followed quickly by a double, extra strong beat as I heard this. My tensed muscle tone left and I could feel my entire body relaxing. It was as if I were with Sam and Francis, in the midst of my loving family. But how could this be? I had only met her, had only been introduced to her!

"After your heroic deed in avenging your father at such a young age, we all in Los Angeles and San Gabriel feel safer in knowing you are part of our defense against the killers in our society. But I'm just as concerned about thieves in our society stealing the Ranchos of our Californios and the little holdings of small families as well. Our Mr. Carlisle over there, supposedly the scion of a Virginian aristocratic family, had a hold over your poor blacksmith, Mr. Micajah Johnson, and forced him to kill your father. Something to do with a nester's family a few years ago.

"You do know Mr. Carlisle, I believe. You came into the saloon together. He is sparking the daughter of Col. Williams, Francisca."

These few sentences drove my amorous thoughts out of my mind. Carlisle! What had he been playing? Acting as if he had no knowledge of the hacienda and blundering around the home when he was actually courting the daughter of the house. And now hearing that Carlisle was actively engaged in the death of my father through using a minion. Learning that his friends supported the truth of Mrs. Rice's tale of the killing of her nester husband just for the water rights of the spring.

I looked again at Laura. How could one so young put this together? Or did all the ladies of Los Angeles know this and we men folk had never thought to discuss it with them in fear of distressing them? And Laura was bold enough at fifteen to mention this to me, the first time we met. I vowed to myself that I would never misplace her trust her trust in me.

"Miss Laura, I thank you for your thoughts on these matters. Please do not discuss this further for it might prove dangerous."

"Carlisle is aware we hold these beliefs. He believes he is so powerful that we women folk do not matter. But he forces Francisca to agree with him for she fears him. He is utterly without redemption. I only hope that Colonel Williams comes to his senses and bans him from his house and friends."

I couldn't tolerate this gathering any longer. There was too much emotion circling around me. I had to get into the open air and ride it off. "Miss Laura, I must go now. May I have the honor of visiting you at your San Gabriel home, *The Locust*? Naturally when your parents are home."

"Yes. Mother is almost always present, along with our parlor maids.

We shall be pleased to greet you any afternoon. You will enjoy my parents for they are worldly and nice."

And with those words, I bid *Adios* to all at the Rancho Santa Ana del Chino, even Carlisle, for I did not wish to alert him to my true feelings and what I had learned during this visit. I totally forgot that the purpose of my attending the gathering of Col. Williams was to meet him and his friends, to further my burgeoning career. But I could only focus my thoughts upon Carlisle, and upon his antithesis, Laura, the heavenly angel.

I pushed Star to a fast trot on the 40 mile trip home for I had to discuss the findings with my brothers. I made the short jog off the Foothill Path to The Monte and down to Lexington where Sam had his small ranch. Fortunately, Frank was visiting too.

I loosened the girth of Star's saddle, and tethered him close to the water trough. I would ride on in an hour or so. Then I hailed the house although their dogs had announced my visit by barking and growling.

"Howdy Sam, Frank. I've got to talk with you."

"Good to see you AJ," Frank, the talkative one responded. "It's been almost a week. Sit down, light up a cheroot and we can palaver."

"It will be more than that. I found out who was behind Pa's killing. It was that humbug Virginian "gentleman," Carlisle. Pa found out that Carlisle had shot that nester, Rice, and forced his wife to leave his homestead. She made her way with her 4 year old daughter to the stage stop at Banning, a two day's hard walk. She almost had to "go on the line" to survive, but she married a sheep herder four days later. As you know, she still lives around here but is scared to say anything.

"I couldn't find out how Carlisle forced poor Micajah Johnson to murder Pa that night but I heard that he did."

"AJ, how did you learn all of this?"

"Women knew about it. They just didn't talk about it. Probably didn't want to put their men folks up against Carlisle and his outlaw vaqueros and have them killed. Laura Evertsen told it to me today out at Don Julian's hacienda and I believe every word she said."

"That's some girl-woman. How did you meet her? She's Evertsen's daughter, only fifteen, and he's been protecting her for years. Watch out there. She's not for the likes of us."

"Boys, I'm goin'a marry her. It's just that she doesn't know it yet.

"She's said she will allow me to visit her at home, the Locust, by the San Gabriel Mission. And I'll be spendin a good deal of my time there. Of all the men in town, she told only me about Carlisle. That's what she believes of me and I'm goin'a live up to it.

"Help me out if you can. I want her."

"We'll help you if we can. What do you want us to do?"

Then Sam, the doer, spoke. "AJ, you should go to the City Attorney, James H. Lander. Tell him what you've heard. He'll investigate and maybe file an indictment for murder against Carlisle in the Rice death. If not, then we'll take action again, this time against Carlisle for Pa's death.

"How sure are you that this information is correct? This is the first time we've heard of it although it certainly sounds true. We've never known why Johnson killed Pa, just that he did. It'll also show your lady that you believed her and did something about it.

"Thanks, Sam. I'll do that tomorrow."


"Mr. Lander, I appreciate your kindness in seeing me…."

"Please call me James, and if you find it agreeable, I'll call you AJ for I know of you and the future you are building both for yourself and for our fair city."

"Thank you, James. I should have spoken with you months ago about this matter when I first heard about it.

"I would like to inquire about Mr. Robert S. Carlisle. I have heard several witnesses speak that they know Carlisle killed that nester, Rice, and then claimed and homesteaded Rice's year round spring for his Rancho. So many people know about it that it is not a secret, just a fact. I also have a witness who will testify that Carlisle is behind the killing of my father, Sheriff Samuel King back in January two years ago. I'm wondering if you could initiate an action against him for these murders."

"AJ, we in this office know about this. In fact, I have tried to go forward on these cases and cannot. Carlisle is so politically powerful, that he is literally impervious to actions of law against him. The County Jury has heard of several cases involving Carlisle, and to date, they have refused to indict him. I am powerless. If you can assist me to indict, I shall be most pleased to do so. But I have not found it possible."

"Thank you, James. Presently, I too, am powerless against him. However, in the future, power may shift and perhaps we can bring him to a late justice at that time.

"Again, thank you very much for allowing me to discuss this with you. Good day."

Again, that same response. Carlisle was just too powerful and had too many powerful friends. Even our City Attorney, James H. Lander, could do nothing against him. But who were these unknown powerful friends?

Just as when Pa died, I must put aside my losses and forage on. But I was not alone, as Sam and Francis were always with me. And now, I knew the brightest star in the firmament, Laura, who was but 15. But I had a distance to go before marriage and must prove that I was worthy of her.

She was the star of Bethlehem, and as in the biblical days, drew me along her shining path as had been the Three Kings. I visited her house next to the San Gabriel Mission, surprised to find no one sparking her even at her tender age. As I was 20, there was no significant age difference and I could wait for her. In conversations with her, I learned she had not expressed a strong interest in either a boy or a man. My presence did not particularly please her family, except for her younger brother who wanted to be a sheriff, but at least I was not run off.

When I was appointed the Under Sheriff to Sheriff Tomas Sanchez, I was greeted as a friend of the family. When I was elected State Representative from Los Angeles County, and met with our Congress in Sacramento, I was treated as an equal, despite the fact of my limited education.

After five long years of wooing, she let me know she was eternally in love with me and I found it was worth every day of waiting to hear her avowal. I had let her know my undying love soon after our initial meeting. For after meeting her, who else was there?

We married New Year's Eve, December 31, 1862. Laura was 20; I was 27 and a man of substance. At the change of the year, rockets burst overhead and pistols and rifles were fired into the heavens celebrating the New Year and our nuptials. We took this as a sign our union was blessed on high. In the years to come, I wondered if these explosions of violence portended man's future course in Los Angeles, or perhaps of the continued War of Northern Aggression?

# Serpent in the Land of Promise

But the play had begun before my arrival in California, the stage had been set, and even if I did not know it, the haunting memories of my future had been placed in motion. Although I don't necessarily believe any of this, still...

Despite later statements of disbelief, Robert S. Carlisle really was the scion of a prominent Virginian family. However, there was no truth to Carlisle's assertion that his ancestral home was Carlisle Castle in Carlisle, Cumbria (E.H.), which had been continuously garrisoned for 2,000 years, or at least since the Romans camped there with a modest fortification.

His actual family of origin was of a later and more prosaic nature; that of descent from a freebooter who was moderately successful in harrying Spanish treasure ships that became separated from their flotillas, and from those who had perished on shallow reefs when driven before sudden Caribbean hurricanes. It was frequently whispered that his Virginian forefathers lit lanterns on their beach during storms, signifying that there was a safe passage for those ships in distress, but these beacons of safety mislead the ships to drive onto sand bars, disgorging valuable cargos and indentured men who could be ransomed.

With the monies from such marginally acceptable endeavors, successful marriages had been arranged and gradually, a measure of societal approval occurred because of accumulation of wealth; and the whispers of the past were smothered. Yet, the spawning of his morally marginal parents produced an eldest son, the heir, Robert S. Carlisle, who outwardly possessed the physical accoutrements of a favored son. He was tall, greater than six feet in height, and slender with a narrow waist and broad shoulders. Legs that were strong and muscular and as the young ladies noted, very shapely in breeches, proved athletic endowed and allowed him to easily best his peers in foot racing and wrestling. Training in the social graces led him to master intricate dancing and riding as a child. Marksmanship with pistol and rifle was merely a matter of practice, and practice he did from an early age.

His comeliness was one of elegance and refinement, aristocratic in bearing and grace. His intelligence allowed him to master not only English and French, but also Latin and ancient Greek, although it is a given that his tutors greatly assisted him in his education. Yet, the elegant, refined young gentlemen appeared strange and distanced, almost detached from his social peers.

For if he were unsuccessful, his father would beat him, but always with a broad strap so his perfect body would not be marked. His accomplishments were achieved with the brutality of animal training. Sweet milk had not flown through the breasts of his mother, for she was brutally beaten if the elder son failed in his training; she could not succor her oldest child for then, she too, was marked as a weakling and punished with deprivation and abuse as was he. There was no love or tenderness in the Carlisle family, only achievement and success which alternated with brutality and viciousness.

His father demanded perfection and winning, even in games of chance; and he was taught tricks of the Mississippi gamblers. He sometimes paired with his father in games played in taverns with other sporting men. When he was a young man of 14, another player dealt from the bottom of the deck; Carlisle's calm exterior demeanor exploded and his Bowie Knife cut through the hand of his opponent, pining it to the table. The knife was extracted only with the help of two men, and one finger was left behind. He was rewarded by his father not with recriminations but with the gift of an experienced lady for the night.

When he was sixteen, several young ladies of good family had to visit distant members of their respective families for many months. This young Adonis who did not possess the rudimentary morals of a tom cat surrounded by ten alley cats in heat, the favored son and heir, had so horrified even his family by these whispered disclosures that he was disowned and sent with a modest purse to seek his fortune elsewhere, preferably in the far west. Actually, he felt as if the young ladies were his just spoils of war, the rewards of his training as taught him earlier by his father. His basic inability to discriminate nuances branded the mark of Beelzebub so strong upon him that his family did not even endow him as a remittance man, although there had been some discussion regarding this. Their conclusion was to have no further ties with him lest his ultimate fall bring down their precarious standing as well. This information was imparted to him in the family library, with several stout servants standing discretely by for protection from any physical eruption.

A year later, Robert S. Carlisle appeared on the overland trail to California with two outstanding horses; two rifles, one in his scabbard, the second, a gold and silver engraved presentation rifle in his baggage; and a handsomely engraved shotgun was also packed in his baggage. A Colt ball and cap revolver was carried in a holster on his hip and a Derringer in a sleeve hideout. All were stolen from his ancestral home at the time of his sudden departure. He had a second purse given to him by his mother and sisters, which was very well filled following a solo surreptitious late evening visit to the family library and the family safe box on the eve of his departure. After all, these accoutrements were his by ancestral right of *primo geniture* and he deserved to possess them.

Robert S. Carlisle appeared in *El Pueblo de Nuestra Senora la Reina de los Angeles de Porciuncula* in 1848 immediately following the annexation of the western territories to the United States. He wore a new suit, and possessed several other elegant suits in his baggage, along with extra boots, all packed on a third thoroughbred. He carried thick wallets of currency and purses filled with gold. He also had a hidden history of killing several wealthy travelers during the course of robberies, but others did not know this and he didn't think about it at all.

He looked at his refuge, the City of Los Angeles, the City of our Queen of the Angels, sometimes known as El Diablo because of the dark deeds done in the night. He was accustomed to earthen streets, but mud huts as houses and stores? Even a mud hotel, La Bella Union Hotel, which had been the capitol building of California for a month under the Mexican flag in 1846, had a ground floor of pounded mud. And here, when sun dried mud was made into thick bricks, they called it adobe and made house walls out of it! They slapped muddy clay on their legs, molding it over the curves of their thighs into elongated, sloppy Cs, half tubes with an up curved, snarling lip. The clay was fired in a rough kiln and then placed on sloping roofs to protect the hovels from rain. They called this fired clay, tile. And only the better buildings of the wealthy had it!

Even the slaves of his ancestral Virginian home lived better than the populace here. Where were the spoils of the gold rush? He would stay, but not long. For months, he had been homesick for the fired brick and polished wood of the mansions of Virginia, the crushed shell lanes shaded with high, overhanging trees, leading to the Porte cochere. There was nothing in Los Angeles to remind him of Virginia. This Pueblo was not for him. Why should he stay?

He soon discovered the reason. This backwards, unsophisticated village misnamed as a city, was owned and ruled by men who lived at least 50 to 100 years in the past. Los Angeles and its county, spread from the sea to the shining Colorado River. Its area was larger than the states of Connecticut, Delaware, Maryland, Massachusetts, New Hampshire, New Jersey and Rhode Island combined! And no-one seemed to be aware of this grand opportunity!

The demarcation between the borders of a house and the street, truthfully only paths between the hovels, was unclear. The yards and streets were both filled with loose animals. One better adobe house on the corner of Calle Principal and the Plaza seemed to have a continuous cock fight in progress in its front yard, the natural spurs of the cocks enhanced by long, sharp spurs of iron, sometimes so long that the cocks cut themselves rather than slashing and killing their opponents.

The filthy dusty path out of the south eastern corner of the Plaza led to a make shift corral which was sometimes filled with cattle, sometimes with a captured brown bear tied to a bull by his back foot, who then fought to the death. There were even primitive bleachers for the occasional bull fight; the crowd could sit while enjoying the toreador, always billed as from Mexico.

But on Sunday evening, the corral was limited to the Yang-na, Gabrielinos and a few descendants of the Pobladores, who had been rounded up by squads of special Indian deputies. They spent Sunday night here in the cattle corral, sleeping off their intoxication, waiting for Monday morning when they were sold to the highest bidder for another week's involuntary work. All, but for the one or two who died overnight in the corral. On the following Saturday evening, their weeks pay was given them in the form of raw brandy, pishibata, at the close of their week's slavery. And thus every Sunday evening, the indentured cycle began anew.

There were only three houses on the Plaza that had clay tile roofs. The others were of wooden beams crossed with branches and the long reeds from the nearby sloughs, then covered with brush and dried grasses, topped off with the brea from the pits along La Cienega. When the hot summer arrived, the brea ran down the adobe sides of the buildings in thick black fingers and it was the unusual hovel where it had been scraped off the walls. The poor had even less, with the walls made of the tulle reeds providing a support for the daubing on of the clay mud. Some inhabitants lived in open fields away from the Plaza, erecting a tulle and mud sided conical tent around a makeshift center pole of a growing bush.

Carlisle's knee high boots were polished daily. The few streets were filled with horse apples and cow pies, which he didn't mind as much as the remains of human waste and animal carcasses. The high boots also kept the packs of mongrel dogs from attacking his legs. He attributed this to his well-placed kicks.

With his resource of stolen goods and monies, and socially supported by his manners trained throughout childhood, he easily posed as a young man of wealth and breeding. He was soon ensconced in the *gente de razon* of the Pueblo, and introduced to the Ton. His unspoken goal was reached when presented to young ladies of wealth. But it was not until 1851 that he knew this was his promised land. In 1851, The United

States Congress passed *"A Bill to Settle Private Land Claims in California"* and established a *Board of Land Commissioners* to adjudicate such claims and granting land patents to the claimants. The passage of these bills confirmed his reasons for remaining in this blighted area and some years after, until he found his desired target, a wealthy family without a strong masculine leader.

He was introduced to a Californiano, Colonel Isaac Williams, the wealthiest land grant holder in the entire state of California, owner of both *Rancho Cucamonga* and the *Rancho Santa Ana del Chino*. It was of particular interest to Carlisle that the Colonel had no living son and only two young legitimate daughters. When Don Isaac suddenly died on September 13, 1856, his older daughter Dona Merced Williams, 17, married the foreman of the Rancho the very next day. It took Carlisle a little big longer, about six months in fact, to marry Don Isaac's youngest daughter, Francisca Williams, who was but 16.

Carlisle immediately began his manipulations to expand his power. He cheated his sister-in-law out of her half ownership (24,000 acres) of *Rancho Santa Ana del Chino*, paying only $500 dollars. He then looked around for other lands to conquer. And of course, it is always easier to do this against the poor and helpless. In addition to the constant ascension against his wife and her weak sister, he moved against his most defenseless neighbors. For example, it was told to me...

The hot, half globe of the rising sun bloodied the tops of the mountains and the knife sharp ridges of their slopes a brilliant red; clefts of the high valleys between them still lay in purple darkness; the curving edges of alluvial plains at their feet glistened as they fanned out and became desert.

Upon the plain, in the false darkness of the dawning day in the summer of 1856, the fitful westward wind blew the seed laden tops of the wild oats and grasses in waves which broke upon the rocky chaparral and thick broad leafed spiny cactus of the low hills bordering the 24,000 acre Chino Ranch. Don Roberto Carlisle led his band of ten men in the early morning darkness, walking the horses and giving them a blow. It was unlikely they could be seen and any dust raised would not be visible. Their quarry was miles distant and most probably still asleep in his mud and stone hut.

The land was unusually dry this summer; Southern California was already experiencing an early draught. Carlisle needed the spring to water his cattle. An omission in the tumultuous last days of Pio Pico's reign left the springs in the low hills bordering his ranch outside the land grant. The oversight became disastrous when the nester filed his homestead and began running sheep. Carlisle needed the water, which, by right, should have been his and the sheep were eating the sweet grasses and shrubs down to the roots, destroying the grazing for years.

Despite the cool morning hours and gentle ride, hours of walking and slow trotting caused both horses and men to sweat from exertion; and the rays from the rising sun penetrated their clothes and warmed their backs. In the dawn, Carlisle raised his right hand and the ten riders stopped. Standing in his stirrups, he stretched and pointed northwest. "There, to the left of the low cliff at the line of the rising sun. See the cottonwoods? That's where the springs are, where we'll find the water and their shack."

Carlisle and his men rode up a gently rounded meandering mound, then down the steeper, water cut bank, and crossed over the wide, dry arroyo of the Santa Ana River. Hoofs did not sink into the ground now, as the dry river bottom was packed firmer than the looser desert sand on the berms of the seasonal river. Riding through the sandy bottom of chaparral, cactus, and an occasional date palm, the acrid, sage scented wind provided some relief from the hot, dry air. Climbing out of the arroyo and riding up-slope for another half hour, they had seen no one, but details of the sod hut were now clear to them.

The walls were stacked rocks, tamped with adobe mud using grass as a binder. Short straight branches framed open rough rectangles covered by stretched translucent cow intestines. The sun illuminated the one room habitation, but objects and persons could not be seen, even as shadows behind the membrane barrier. Flat river rocks from the arroyo placed on the ground served as the door threshold; stacked high, they built the two retaining sides of the door opening; and then, placed above the cottonwood lintel, other flat rocks provided strength for the roof. A stiff dried cowhide was permanently tied to the wooden lintel and to the left side of the door opening, serving as a wind break and a door for protection when lashed tightly. Rawhide thongs were punched through the hide's right edge and laced tightly closed to protect the inhabitants from the denizens of the night. The silhouette of the brush and thick sod roof blended into the hill landscape rising behind the hut, broken by only a rock chimney that poked its flu above the line of the roof. A poor but hard working man had built this dwelling far from any neighbor, and had almost succeeded in hiding it from others.

The riders stopped a hundred feet away in a shallow draw protected by an outcropping of rock a little higher than the ground of the sod house. Carlisle dismounted and removed his Springfield from its scabbard. He surreptitiously held it pointing downward in his right hand. He strode stiffly toward the cabin always keeping his left flank forward which obscured his right arm and the rifle. At fifty feet he yelled, "Come out'a there thief or we'll burn your house down!"

After a moment, a child started wailing and crying. Then a high-pitched, shaky voice of the nester came from inside the sod house. "I ain't no thief and this here is my land! Get off of it! God fearing people know you and know what you'r doin!"

"Get out of there and we'll leave your woman and brat alone! I want to talk to you, man to man!"

"I filed on this here piece at the land office, proper like. It's mine and in my name, Rice. You got no call to talk to me like this!"

Don Roberto motioned to his fighting hand Breed to circle around the hut. Breed crawled forward using the outcropping as concealment until he reached the rear of the hut where there were no windows.

Breed scratched a Lucifer on a smooth hard rock; it sputtered and smelled of brimstone as it caught fire. He stuck the lit Lucifer between dry twigs until they caught fire. Then he pushed the small fire closer to the back wall and placed dry branches over the flame. When they blazed, he threw in larger branches and the flames quickly reached the roof. Smoke began to obscure the form of the sod house. He quickly added less seasoned, green wood that produced more smoke.

"Nester, are you comin' out now? Your house will fry you all!"

The nester untied the lacings of the cowhide door. Coughing, he sidled out to his left, away from the smoking house. His wife and five year old daughter came out choking, holding cloths over their mouths and moved to his right. Carlisle's piercing whistle carried to the back of the shack. Breed kicked the burning and smoking wood away from the walls and crouching, ran around the left side of the shack to the front.

"Nester, you rustled them cows and used their hides for your shack. We're gonna hang you for rustlin'. Come forward and meet your maker!"

"There weren't no brand on that old maverick. It belonged to no one. Look at the back side of the hide. You're lying". The nester ran forward, wearing just his boots, pants and a coat. He reached into his coat pocket for his old Colt.

Don Roberto lifted his left hand from his gun belt as a distraction and swiveled his concealed rifle hidden by his right side, up to the horizontal. In the same motion, he aimed and fired at the nester. The report was long and drawn out, for Breed and the other riders had also fired when the nester reached for his pistol. The nester crumpled to the ground and the only sounds heard in the silence after the guns were his death rattles and jerking leg movements as his clodhoppers beat the earth in a tattoo of death, the *danse macabre*. His clenched mouth grinned in the rictus of death, and his body stank.

"You. Woman. Take your brat and go! If you're not gone in 10 minutes, you'll join your man! We'll take care of him for you."

"Where will I go? I ain't got no one. I got no money."

"There's a stage at Banning. You can walk there in two days. Get moving!"


"Yes Sir, it was only told to me. But from what we soon learned about Mr. Robert S. Carlisle, it was all true."

# Golden Horse, Gold Doubloons

The sound that slammed against the rattling windows of my law office on Main Street just south of the Plaza that fall morning of 1860 seemed a combination of an elephant passing gas and a hippopotamus eructating. A huge shadow with a small head bobbing up and down like a ball on the end of a marionette string, projected clearly on my inside wall; some ancient Indian Legend must have come down from the mountains. Dragging my four-pound Dragoon from its covered envelope on the wall peg behind my desk, I ran out into the street.

Men in Army uniforms were riding side saddle, one leg up and around an unusual pommel on a very different saddle on smelly, humpbacked creatures ambling in single file down Main Street and through the Plaza. Flies were buzzing around this desert caravan and their riders. The long and tall monsters with ungainly springing necks and small heads, bobbing as if hung on invisible marionette strings, would hawk and spit accurately into the crowd. One creature extended its foul mouth with hardened thick blubbery lips flicking out a horny tongue and in one lick, tore the sweaty shirt off the back of a muleskinner. The man ducked and twisted out of the creature's horny jaw with backward facing rasps on its tongue, saving the skin on his back from a flaying. Thick multicolored blankets were cinched on the animals as if Jacob had lost all of his coats somewhere in the Californian deserts and they had been scavenged by these desperate wanderers; water skins and other articles hung and jangled as the tired creatures lumbered down the dusty street.

The brutes could not even walk without drawing attention to their jointed legs and footpads. Spectacle, sound, and stench rose from this parade; the shouting spectators responded with overwhelming cries and noises.

These must be our "*ships of the desert*," the U.S. Army Camel Corps, conceived by our Secretary of War, The Honorable Jefferson Davis, finally braving the sight of others by leaving their isolated headquarters where they were hidden at Fort Tejon on their way to Drum Barracks in Wilmington. Hopefully, Jefferson's other decisions would prove more opportune in the future.

I pushed the Dragoon under my belt on the left, covered it with my waistcoat, and as the caravan continued south towards Fort Drum, my head slowly swiveled left, back over the street to the Plaza and suddenly, next to me was that darned Carlisle with Breed at his side.

"Good afternoon, Consular," said Carlisle jostling my left side. "Congratulations upon your new positions as Deputy City Attorney and Under Sheriff."

"This is a fascinating sight," he continued, "but not as interesting as one that will present itself here at the Pueblo in a few months. Are you a gambling man?"

"Sir, I have nothing to say to you," I responded, slowing turning my head and shoulders to the right, removing him from my sight and hopefully from further speaking.

Don Roberto continued as if he had the right to speak with me.

"I'm traveling with my friend, Don Jose Antonio Andreas Sepulveda, to San Francisco. He has purchased an Australian mare, Black Swan, a genuine English thoroughbred whose lineage can be traced back to the sire of all English thoroughbreds, Godolphin Arabian. Don Jose has never seen Black Swan but his reputation says he is unbeatable. Don Jose is willing to wager his Ranchos San Joaquin and Palos Verdes that are immediately adjacent to my Rancho Santa Ana del Chino that his new horse will beat any horse in California. And he will make this wager even before he sees his new horse.

"We shall go to the docks at San Francisco and watch Black Swan disembark. Don Jose's trainer, Bill Brady, will bring him overland to Los Angeles. If Don Pio Pico is brave enough, we shall race Black Swan against his California champion, Sarco, who is, after all, just another mustang from a cattle ranch in Sonora. And we will win!"

I lost my control over this naked exposure of the "real", conniving Carlisle.

"Sir, your friend, Don Pio Pico, was the Governor of Alta California and an earlier Governor of California deeded your Chino Rancho to the Lugo family which descended to the wife of Colonel Isaac Williams. He, as he lay dying, willed this Rancho to his youngest    ** daughter, your future 16 year old wife, as her dowry. Without that, you would have remained just another penniless adventurer in a foreign land. Don't turn your back on Don Pio and Don Pedro Carrillo now that the *Californios* are no longer the power in our new state! Or are you just an Americanized Sydney Duck, but one who has exchanged the docks of San Francisco for the Los Angeles Plaza?"

Carlisle continued without directly answering me, as if it were important that I understand his position.

"Family interests and friends frequently change. Don Jose Sepulveda, his son-in-law, Tom Mott, Black Swan's trainer Bill Brady, and I, for I too, own a part interest in Black Swan, will run our horse against Sarco. If you are a friend of Don Pio Pico, see to it that Sarco is ready. But Sarco has no chance of winning."

Carlisle's statement struck me as hard as a blow to my stomach. I knew the man was dishonest and could not be trusted. But here again, he paraded as a gentleman amongst the finest *Californios* who could not distinguish him from other, honorable Anglos. What was he planning?

I asked myself, "How could Black Swan win against Sarco?" Sarco was originally from Mexico, a Sonorian mustang of history from the Mexican and Californian cattle ranches, a horse descended from the horse of the *Conquistadores*. A Californian horse that had never lost a race, which had won all major distances up to several leagues and was invincible. What was Carlisle's trick? I knew he had to have one!

That night in the dining room of the Bella Union Hotel, the challenge

was presented in a more gentlemanly manner by Don Jose Antonio
Andreas Sepulveda. When Don Jose rose from the table as if about to
present a toast, I saw him as a short man whose feet in stirrups, would
barely reach down to the flank of a medium sized horse. His slender
erect body was derived from his meager Spanish ancestry that was
overwhelmed with generations of Indio. His chin was held high, and the
cruel Aztec in his face projected his overall presence. A sharp, beaked
nose divided the mask, making one wonder if his eyes saw forward
or lateral as a bird of prey. When he stared, the quaking entity of his
scrutiny knew the piercing eyes were drilling through his head and
into his thoughts. His side burns were heavy, with straight black hair,
becoming a dark coppery tarnished bronze as they merged into almost
unruly mutton chops. He slowly moved his eyes which were followed by
his turning head, to scrutinize all diners, dominating them one by one.

Then I heard Don Jose gently bell his crystal glass with a sterling
knife.

"I will toast my close Amigo, Don Pio Pico, Governor of Alta
California, Grantor of my Ranchos, Godfather of my children and my
children's children with the following act of friendship. I have purchased
an Arabian who should be named Pegasus, as she was created by the
Gods and drinks the wind as she floats over our earth. I would like to
introduce the Black Swan to our people in a *charreria*, a tradition which
goes back in history to the time when our forefathers brought gallant
steeds to the new world and conquered New Spain, as *gente de raison*.
Would you honor us by racing your Sarco, a descendent of those horses
which bravely accompanied our *conquistadores*, a mustang of history from
our Sonorian and Californian Ranchos in a *charreada*?"

Don Pio Pico, the son of an army sergeant, sat on the opposite side
of the table. His deep voice and huge laugh and smile lines, cast shadows
onto his gleaming burnished mahogany visage, and disclosed his love
of life. His nose, flat and broadened at the tip, topped with three small
round bumps, hinted of African heritage as did his slightly protuberant
fleshy lips; already at age 59, his high brow was marked by hair that
showed salt and pepper. Everyone in the room was pleased to see him,
for all knew his generosity, most of them as personal recipients. As they

applauded him, they recalled and whispered to one another how Don Pio had carried his cousin, Maria Carrillo, away from her unwanted suitor, Governor Echeandia of Alta California, to her betrothed, Captain Fitch, who was awaiting their surreptitious arrival at the Point Loma Harbor. With a smile, and an assist from his ivory handled cane carved in the shape of a cancan dancer's leg, Don Pio Pico rose, his glass lifted high as he turned and saluted all present.

"My dear Amigo, Don Jose. You are a man from whom all goodness flows. Our entire world, here in the southern part of the great state of Alta California, benefits from your largesse's. We know and love you and your family from the time your forefathers rode with the *conquistadores* upon foreign shores. Under your family's guidance, I, who was born under a bush outside the walls of San Gabriel Mission, a child of the *Pobledores*, have twice risen to be governor of Alta California under the flag of Mexico, in 1832 and again in 1845. This very hotel, the Bella Union, that was once our State Capitol building in 1845, is like us. We can remember when it was but one story with a dirt floor, and today, just as we are, it is modern, with a stone floor and two stories. It is an honor for our Sarco, a dear child from the legacy of the Conquistadors, to race against your Arabian, a stranger to our shores as once, we all were."

"Don Jose, if you are in agreement, let our many friends meet and determine the rules and conditions for the race."

"My dear friend, Don Pio. Certainly we should let our friends determine an honorable race. Are we not all *Californios*? Do we not share the same families and history? Please let it happen."

I stood with the others and listened silently. Both my friends were true and honest men. But such men are often naïve in their trust. I knew Carlisle. Although he too, had friends, they were beholden to him through nefarious schemes. How was he planning to subvert the *Californios* and obtain advantage in the contest between two champion horses? Who or what was this Arabian, the modern Pegasus who drank the wind as he flowed over the land? I had to see him. I would travel to the docks of San Francisco and secretly observe him as he disembarked.

I was concerned about Carlisle and would do anything to bring him down. He had cheated that poor Rice woman out of her widow's mite after killing her husband. And who really knew all his crimes?

I left my brothers Samuel Houston and Francis Marion, both deputy sheriffs, to assist Sheriff Tomas Sanchez in my duties as Under Sheriff; my position as City Attorney could tolerate a short absence.

I caught the Butterfield Stage the very next morning.


I was dockside when Black Swan disembarked. I had assumed this modern Pegasus was a stallion but she was a mare! Don Jose Sepulveda had not misspoken when he described Black Swan using a female pronoun. Who had ever heard of a mare racing? Not in California. Never! Black Swan tottered slowly down the gangplank in an excessively careful manner, almost stumbling, determinedly placing one foot in front of the other. She was not impressive; a small, gaunt, visibly emaciated horse with hanging, folded skin as if she had lost all fat and muscle. Her gait was unsteady and wide; she was unable to balance! It was no wonder she couldn't walk when one observed her short, skinny legs with bony, knobby knees. Her head hung low as if it were too heavy for her long, emaciated neck. Her coat was not lustrous but a mangy dull, an almost moth-eaten, sickly appearance with many shiny areas of skin where all hair had been lost. There was no life in this tepid mare; there was no way this horse could beat Sarco. She couldn't walk, much less run.

Then I noticed Ito, a gray gelding who was also from the same Australian stable, disembarking. He stepped lively down the gangplank although a bit unsteady from the months-long voyage. Was this the secret? Were the two to be switched? But how? A gelding and a mare?

I remained in San Francisco the next month and watched the training of the two horses from Australia. Both were trained by Bill Brady and Tom Mott. In two weeks, Ito was racing and even winning one-mile heats. Then the gelding was matched against Black Swan for $10,000 at the Pioneer Jockey Club in San Francisco. Ito won! What could be going on? Black Swan appeared little better health wise than I had seen her a month earlier. This was more than just the need to recover from sea voyage. I learned she had been sick throughout the voyage and arrived in a listless condition. Previously, she had been described as gentle and responsive.

Was this because there was no "fire" in her?

In a month, when Black Swan sufficiently recovered for the land trip to Los Angeles, I was present when my friend Don Jose gently spoke with his trainer, Bill Brady.

"Trusted friend, take my beautiful princess and bring her to me in Los Angeles, sound in heart and body. Be as gentle as if she were your youngest daughter."

Although I immediately returned to my duties in Los Angeles, it was weeks before the Black Swan reached the outlying areas of our fair city. I was one of those who lined the El Camino Real as Black Swan reached Los Angeles. Bill Brady had gently ridden her the 500 miles to Los Angeles, always choosing the easiest route with the softest of paths. If the way were stony, Brady dismounted and walked her; whenever possible, the fallen Pegasus was walked on the coastal beach sands in shallow water to protect her hooves and slowly build her strength as she certainly "could not drink the winds as she floated over our earth."

Supporters loudly cheered the small group of horsemen through Los Angeles on their way to the Sepulveda stables. I personally observed that Black Swan was still experiencing the effects of the long sea voyage and she could barely carry Brady. Her loose skin fell in folds along her bent neck and withers, her skinny legs were short with large knobby joints joined by short bones, and her steps were still short and listless. Her eyes were dull and unintelligent, not bright and inquisitive as they should have been for a horse of her stature and reputation. How could she compete against Sarco or even the other local horses in the promised *charreada*? And where was Ito who apparently had not made the journey south? What was Carlisle's plan to win the richest race in history?

I recognized the educated, patronizing haughty voice immediately. Carlisle had again appeared on my left side without my observing him until his hand brushed my left side.

"Counselor," he said, "I'm pleased to see you. I saw you on the docks at San Francisco but the crowd was too great to greet you. What do you think of Black Swan now?

"And I notice you still carry your Dragoon in a shoulder holster on your left side."

"Don't even hint that you are threatening me! My father was murdered in this Plaza one night and I soon made the murderer pay for it. But there are still many questions unanswered. Perhaps you could assist if you would."

"No, I cannot." And then Carlisle continued.

"But counselor, what do you think of our horse, Black Swan?"

I responded truthfully. "She is a sorry horse. Lifeless. Small, with big bones but without muscles, and with short legs that cannot run. Swan, indeed! More like a mole with her head underground. She cannot even carry her head high! She certainly can't carry the weight of a rider for the distance. I don't approve of men running horses to death just to win a race. And she won't even win!

"How can you even think of running her? She couldn't even beat Ito on a short mile course!

"And where is Ito?"

"Counselor, look around. Every supporter of Sarco is here. And they all believe what you believe. We've had runners monitoring Black Swan's progress and reporting to us. We let everyone know when she would arrive in Los Angeles, especially those who are backing Sarco. And they all think we are foolish to race Black Swan. Just look at them betting! But you'll see!"

What was the plan? Was Carlyle really going to substitute Ito? But how? A gelding cannot be disguised as a mare.


Don Pio Pico requested that I join him and his principal aids in the negotiations for the race. Although an Anglo, I was known for supporting the *Californios*, and now spoke excellent Spanish, knew horses, and was an Under Sheriff as well as a Deputy City Attorney practicing law. Personally, I was pleased to be involved as I was still looking for the trick that must be present if Carlisle were involved.

Negotiations were conducted in the neutral Grand Salon of the Bella Union Hotel. Don Pio Pico and his principal aids were sitting on one side of the room; Don Jose Sepulveda and his principal aids, including Don Roberto Carlisle as he was now known, were in chairs against the wall on the other side. The meetings were conducted with the formality of the *Grandee Espana*; the *Californios* were formally attired in their native splendor and I even wore my claw hammer. Every minute detail of the race was given the full weight of consideration. After many afternoon sessions for more than a month, our two groups finally agreed upon the general rules.

The race would be run on a Sunday, three months following acceptance of the rules by both parties. Owners of other horses would simply have to agree if they were to enter. Everyone knew the race was between the two principles and unless a miracle happened, either Sarco or Black Swan would win. The familiar agreement was similar to those of many prior races between these two friends.

It was the love of gambling, the excitement of the wager, the unknown which drove them. And the bet agreed upon was tremendous- the largest amount in the history of the state: gold, livestock and even ranches. Each principal party was to have present for immediate delivery after the race; $25,000 dollars in gold, the new octagon slugs minted in San Francisco, 500 horses and 500 mares, 500 heifers and 500 calves, and 500 sheep, along with small ranches of equal value. The livestock was to be penned near the finish line, the winner to take them following the race; the gold was given to the Mayor of Los Angeles to hold until the winner was decided.

Then the tall, handsome 33 year old Don Roberto stood, and received recognition from the two families. Carlisle was a most impressive man (I refuse to think of the false description of gentleman). His presence was made even more grave by his preened long wavy black hair folded over the upper lobe of his ears, continuing down and forward on both his upper and lower jaws, meeting his mustache and then swelling into a full beard instead of a simple goatee; one would never dare to say it appeared as if it were a goat's beard. This accentuated his dark heavy eyebrows and his Roman nose.

He spoke with a deep, mellifluous voice, appropriate for his stature. His Spanish had the accent of a slight southern drawl with the Virginian flatness.

"Gentlemen, neighbors, friends. We have gathered here to set the rules by which a fair race should be conducted. Both of these horses are outstanding representatives of their lineage, one of Sonorian, the other of Arabian heritage. Let us develop a standard that will stand for the ages, that other races can only venerate.

"Sarco is a golden horse from the *Conquistadores*, one whose blood and bones has carried his lineage from Spain to New Spain, through Mexico and Sonora, to our fair lands of Alta California. We, *Californios*, can be proud of him and his heritage, for they have enabled us to survive in our beauteous country, against *Indios* and pestilence, against draught and flood. We know his strength and his endurance. Let Sarco again demonstrate that strength!

"But what of Black Swan? A mare?

"She comes to us with her heritage out of Arabia, a desert. We Spanish remember when the hordes swarmed out of that Dark Continent and ruled us for centuries, until finally, we overcame them and ejected those foreign Bedouin nomads. Yet, the Black Swan too, so they say, is a champion. Let her prove it!"

Murmuring sounds came from the Grandees, along with shoes pounding the floor and hands beating the arms of the chairs in approval of the fiery speech. Carlisle spoke well but since when was he of Spanish heritage? And he certainly wasn't a "Don"-just a foreign adventurer who married a very young defenseless child of a Californio.

Don Roberto stood motionless until the noise died away. He then continued.

"I would suggest a lengthy course, to be run in view of all our people. Let the horses race on a wide street. Then circle and return to cross the starting line for the finish. For all to see." After this extemporaneous delivery, Carlisle sat down although the murmuring in the Grand Saloon intensified.

What was he trying to do? What was his objective? It appeared as if he were inciting the crowd of both contingencies against Black Swan! I just couldn't figure it out!

The Grandees soon determined the location and length of the course.

The race would begin at the southern city limits, on San Pedro Street and 7th Ave, just south of the Plaza. The horses would run south on San Pedro Street through the newer section of Los Angeles for 1½ leagues, turn around a post set in the middle of the dusty road, and race back to the starting line. It was a full course of 3 leagues or about 9 ½ miles. There was no mention as to the weight either horse would carry. As the race was long, it was agreed that each side could use other, non-competing riders, to whip their racehorse on, a not unusual stipulation for a long race.

What had been the objective of Carlisle's inciting speech? I couldn't figure it out. Black Swan could not run the distance, especially against Sarco.

My position as Under Sheriff and City Attorney allowed me to control my time and I decided to observe the two horses in training. Perhaps the secret lay here; a switch of Ito for Black Swan?

Sarco was being trained the same way as all California racehorses. That is, without training! None! The *Californios* were unaware of the concept of training for a contest. All *Charreada* were informal and betting was between friends or at least, acquaintances. All California horses were considered to be in race condition at all times and thus, they did not need further training. So, golden Sarco received no training or conditioning. He looked powerful and he was powerful, with long muscular legs producing an exceptionally long stride, a known trait in Sonorian mustangs. And he was bigger than the usual range mustang, longer and higher. But could he win such a long race? But then, how could Black Swan?

It was assumed that Black Swan was turned out to pasture the day of her arrival at Palos Verdes, in order to overcome the pneumonia contracted on the long damp sea voyage. After all, there were more than four months before the race.

Black Swan healed in the gentle warm climate, moderated by the warm ocean. My early morning riding on the Rancho Palos Verdes revealed that as her strength increased, she began to run, first slowly without a rider, then with gentle riding. Bill Brady conditioned her gradually but ever more intensively. A beloved child could not have received better care. Initially, she was walked and later, slowly run in the gentle surf of Santa Monica Bay. She even went swimming when the surf was low and the waves were gentle. Weeks later, as her strength and endurance grew, I had to observe at night, as Black Swan was exercised and run hard only during the dark and then again, during the very early morning hours. Her gradually increasing speed went unnoticed by others. As the race date approached, she became unbelievably fast, and displayed great endurance. There was no way Star and I could keep up with her even for short distances. But there had to be more than mere breeding and training behind Carlisle's scheme.

Suddenly, the race became the most talked about event of the year, from the Pacific Ocean to the banks of the Colorado River, from the Mexican Border to San Francisco and beyond, even to the gold camps of Hang Town and the Sierras. Every newspaper focused on the race, and were filled with stories of the wagering, most of them favoring our golden Sarco with the odds against Black Swan. Bets were made through the newspapers, and curriers raced from hamlet to town, bearing gold or deeds to mines, farms and ranches. Weeks before the actual race, the amount of money bet was the greatest in the history of California. Everyone who could, gathered their gold and hurried to Los Angeles to see the race, those who could not, bet locally.

The night before the race was hot and dry with only a light east wind. Perfect weather was the belief…

I awoke at five in my house on Breed Street, just West of Main, and rode my horse to the large barn by 7th and San Pedro. The great Fiesta day had dawned with a clear sky and high white clouds overhead. I was lucky to have secured a stall there the previous night. Long before daybreak, all trails and roads to Los Angeles were crowded with cowboys and ranchers riding their horses, while others rode donkeys and mules. Squeaking and even shrieking *Carretas*, with their two high wheels made of slabs of oak, were loaded with families. Pulled by pairs of oxen with their common yoke attached to their short horns, they slowly made their way down the road and paths toward the Plaza of Los Angeles. So many children were running and playing on their way to the race that their way was frequently blocked. But most of the crowd walked on the side of the paths, through the fields of yellow mustard.

Light easterly breezes began to blow and a few white clouds scudded west across the sky and disappeared toward the ocean. Haze soon blurred the air from horizon to horizon and the wind increased. By 10a.m., the wind swept loose dust and sand into the air. A monster dust cloud now covered the bowl of the world from all horizons. Even the mountains had disappeared. The sun was gone, the bowl masked by yellow gloom. The dreaded *Santana*, The Devils Wind, howled in from the eastern desert! It blew as hard as 50-60 miles per hour with gusts of wind whipping up to 80 miles per hour, sweeping up dirt and dried soil into the air, forcing itself down the canyons of Los Angeles created by the high, two story buildings. Was this a sand storm from the Arabian Peninsula heralding the presence of its favored child?

Banshee cries of the Santana were heard as the winds fingered the doors and windows like stops on a flute, causing the wind to moan and cry. Children scattered and could not hear the shouts of their mothers. Skirts were blown high and parasols flew with the winds. Sombreros danced in the skies. Bushes and dried corn stalks came flying out of the cloud, spearing the crowd. Worse yet, sand was striking hands and faces.

Backs were turned toward the wind. Eyes had to be closed and covered in order to protect vision. Clothing was pulled up to cover mouths so one could breath air rather than to eat dust. Riders dismounted and covered the head of their horses with sombreros or serapes. Oxen harnessed to the carretas turned toward the west so as to protect their heads, and could not be forced to move, especially if they had stopped in the wind shadow of a building. Not only did the dust create the need to clear one's throat, it dried out all moisture. One could only cough and hack.

Suddenly, the winds of the Santana abated; Los Angeles was now truly a waterless desert for the small Los Angeles River had disappeared under dust and sand, and any uncovered *Zanja* were filled to the top with debris. Small dust devils continued to dance in The Plaza and down San Pedro Street. The day was hot and dry, and without a breath of moisture.

The morning appearance of the Santana delayed but stopped neither the gathering nor the gambling. The holiday atmosphere continued. Soon, The Plaza and South San Pedro Street were crowded with street venders hawking their tamales, hot tortillas, chili rellenos, fruits, vegetables, nuts, candies and especially drinks. Groups of bettors were everywhere, usually in clusters of supporters for Sarca or the Black Swan.

Senora Francisca Sepulveda, wife of Don Jose Sepulveda, was driven in her majestic two-oak wheeled carreta, pulled by magnificent white oxen, to the area of their supporters. Because of the Sepulvedas' great wealth, expensive tallow had been applied to the single wooden axel before the journey and even during the trip. Her carreta was the only one that did not squeak. Here, Senora Francisca sat high on a gilded chair fastened to the floor in the middle of her carreta, which was festooned with bright colored cloth ribbons and bunting, and carried a cloth top on a wooden frame to protect her from the sun.

Senora Francisca was an aristocrat, a queen in the true sense; with the history and wealth of the Sepulveda family, their bon ton, her haughty carriage and costume complete even to the tiara upon her hair, the gilded golden throne upon the carreta, and the festive cloth top shielding her from the sun. Her devoted subjects milled about the carreta, a retinue of servants and friends. She carried a large heavy leather bag on her lap, which did not blow even in the gusting winds. She reached into her bag without looking and pretentiously distributed a fortune in $50 gold slugs to her servants, and then to the crowd.

"Here my friends. Take these golden octagons. Bet them on our Black Swan and they will multiply. This is our future in Alta California!"

The crowd ran to the purveyors of chance, pushing others in their hurry to bet. For as the time neared for the race, gambling had become more intense, increasing as the force of the dry Santana winds decreased. Alcohol flowed, bets increased, and even small ranches were wagered. It was the most intense gambling in the history of California with the focus of all bets between Sarco and Black Swan.

Other horses were simply not considered. Was this the secret trick? Was Ito running as a local horse? But then, where was the money? How could Carlisle win?

But wait! All bets were placed on the winner of the race, not horse against horse. The winner of the race would take away the fortune, and an outsider could do it!

I hurried to the stables. Sarco was being led to the starting line. Big and beautiful with a shiny, brushed copper colored coat. He positively gleamed in the sun despite the dry heat of the Santana. His legs were long and sturdy, heavily muscled from the hocks up to the high shoulders, bunched with more muscle. Never was there a horse so beautiful or so strong and a feeling of awe flowed through the crowd. The odds against Black Swan increased at the sight of this golden conqueror.

His rider was Jose Martinez, an exceptionally strong man, the finest vaquero from Don Pio's Ranchos of San Fernando, Santa Margarita and Las Flores, and the champion of many charreadas. His shoulders were broad and heavily muscled; his strong thighs made even his leather chaps bulge. One could believe that he could carry Sarca across the finish line if necessary. He was outfitted with a vest covered with silver medallions, and his chaps were studded with two rows of thick silver medallions down their sides. Even his California spurs were silver and gold and his sombrero wore a band of woven silver.

He rode a sturdy, engraved Californian saddle, crafted from a hand shaped wooden saddletree with bronze reinforcements. After the padding was covered with hand tooled leather, it was festooned with shiny silver medallions artistically inserted around glittering jewels; the fender and stirrup leather, the protective tapadero, all were of carved and tooled leather covered with gold and silver. The entire rigging was designed to match and compliment, right down to his spurs. The bullion alone was worth a fortune. Horse and rider sparkled and glistened in the late morning sun as they pranced towards the starting line. Even the two overlapping festive saddle blankets were patterned with woven gold and silver threads on the exposed upper sides. How could any horse even dare to compete with such a magnificent figure as the golden Sarco, the best mixture of the Barb and Spanish horses ever seen, and his equally magnificent rider, Jose Martinez, who glistened in the sun and lacked only the ceremonial sword of the conquistadores to be outfitted completely?

But where was the black mare, the Black Swan?

I walked closer to her stable to ensure it would not be Ito who raced this day for her.

At the starting line, Don Jose gestured and his trainer, Tom Mott gently led Black Swan from her stable. Her black coat glistened as if it were fluid obsidian, moving when the underlying muscles contracted, and reflecting the sunlight in brilliant arcs. She had been dowsed with buckets of water and was thoroughly wet, although perfectly curried with every hair laid back. Her head no longer hung low on an emaciated neck. The neck, now muscular and arched in swanlike curves, proudly carried her head high and tilted up, reaching forward for air as if to take wing. Even her tail was held high, as if balancing her body for flying. Black Swan was an appropriate name! The short leg bones with big joints were now cloaked with incredible musculature. Her rump was high and rounded, ready to leap forward for hours if need be. Her walking gait from the stable to the starting line disclosed she was a natural long distant runner who could float on the air. She was not as high as Sarco but was even more heavily muscled, a long, low horse built for running.

The dry heat of the Santana did not affect this daughter of the Arabian and Australian deserts. She was not even perspiring! But how could one really be certain as her coat was so damp? She then pissed and her passed water was odorless and colorless. Remarkable!

But what about the old superstition that if a horse relieved himself before the race, one should not bet him to win? But perhaps with a mare, it was a lucky charm!

A stable boy sponged out her mouth and washed around her nostrils with water. He reached into his pocket for a cloth, and polished her hoofs with a drop of oil until they shone brighter than Sarco's trappings of silver and gold.

And again, suddenly there was Carlisle with his cultured Virginian voice on my left side. How was he able to sneak up on me all the time? And why always on my left side?

"Good afternoon, counselor. I hope you and your friends took my advice and trained Sarco well. He'll certainly need it today. Have you seen Black Swan?"

He knew I had. He must have seen me closely evaluating her as she was led to the starting line.

"Why yes I have. A beautiful horse but why is she without a saddle? Is your rider riding bareback?"

"No, counselor. Look again!"

I quickly glanced, and my second look disclosed she was not bareback but had a black horse pad on her back. There was also a narrow black piece of leather on her back, which had thin black leather straps connected to bare metal stirrups outside the cinch. The leather was burnished and was not easily seen at first glance-it was the same gleaming black as the mares' glossy wet coat.

"What is that thing? Certainly couldn't ride that in cow country. The cactus would rip your legs right off. The stirrups are so short and weak, they're useless! And it's so small that even a child cannot safely sit on it."

"It's a racing saddle, a black Australian racing saddle. They use it in all their races. And wait until you see our jockey!"

The saddle must have weighed less than three pounds with the stirrups, whereas Sarco's Californian saddle itself, was at least 50 pounds, without the weight of the silver and gold medallions and inlays of the heavy Mexican stirrups built for the bush.

The feeling of superiority of the supporters of the Picos and Carrillos began to waiver and doubts about the outcome began to be expressed. The odds against Black Swan dropped rapidly. But where was her jockey?

Don Jose again gestured and the jockey of Black Swan appeared at the stable doorway. He was either a midget or a very small boy outfitted in black silks with a cap turned backwards. And he was black! The murmur of the crowd increased, along with the excitement. There had never been such a race as this in California or anywhere else. The supporters of the Pico's were openly worried now. How could their magnificent horse win against a black jockey on a black horse? They had appeared with the Santana- Black Devils riding with The Devil Wind!

The Chief Official of the race climbed to the stand where the principal parties and their families were seated, although all were standing now. He raised his hand requesting silence and the murmur of the crowd lessoned.

"Senores and Senoras, please remain quiet until the start is called."

The horses were led to the starting line; the riders were assisted in mounting by their trainers. Both riders assumed a position in their stirrups, crouching forward; neither sat. The Chief Official raised his right hand, then stiffly dropped it as if completing a military salute as he cried, "Santiago!" the battle cry of Cortez and his warriors as they conquered New Spain. Sarco was off and running. Black Swan startled by the unaccustomed cry and screaming of the crowd, reared high on her hind legs, then dropped down onto four feet in a crouch as her jockey regained full control, leapt forward and began running, already six lengths in the rear.

Pico outriders ran their horses with Sarco and began lashing him immediately. Sarco was off to an early lead and the outriders continuously whipped him so he would add to his lead. Even then, even with his long strides that had conquered all other horses, he gained but little.

No one whipped Black Swan and she had no outriders. Her jockey held his riding crop in his right hand but did not use it.

I was riding along the San Pedro Street as fast as my horse would go but had to stop at the crest of a small rise about three miles into the race. All five horses, Black Swan, Sarco, and the three other entries that were racing, were far ahead of me. I could barely see them in the cloud of dust raised by the racing horses and the outriders whipping them. Soon the spectators at the starting line could not distinguish which horse was the leader amidst the dust raised by the morning Santana, dust devils, outriders, racers and spectators. Even before the race had started, men and boys, and some girls too, had climbed to the tarred roofs of the adobe houses for better viewing. Others climbed higher into the trees, perched on branches that sometimes broke, catapulting the spectators to the ground.

Sarco and Black Swan slowly drew away from the following crowd and I could see Sarco and Black Swan were neck and neck when they reached the post at the half way mark. Both horses had slowed down from the long, fast race and both wanted to gallop past the post without turning. Black Swan slowed as her jockey pulled hard on the left rein across her neck, forcing her to begin the counterclockwise turn. Tom Mott stepped from behind the post, carefully grabbed her reins delaying her in the middle of the tight turn when she was at her slowest. While running alongside her, he wiped her muzzle and foaming mouth with a wet sponge and slapped her powerful rump. She started running hard again, and gained more momentum when she was splashed with buckets of cooling water by the Pico vaqueros.

Black Swan raced on tirelessly. Now, her jockey began whipping her and jabbing his spurs into her hide. Her speed increased. Sarco's lead was decreased slightly at every flowing stride. Black Swan steadily closed the gap; the dryness of the Santana had no effect upon her. Her gait was so even and smooth that her body remained level; it appeared as if she were floating and soaring on the wind as if she were a hawk, and we almost expected her to soon leave the ground altogether, her nose outstretched, nostrils flared and channeling the air directly to her lungs. The black jockey had not sat upon his saddle; he had two pointed throughout the race. He sat firmly in the air, thighs parallel to the ground, fixed about six inches above his horse, without his body bobbing or dipping, as if he too were riding the wind!

The outriders running in the fields of yellow mustard raised so much dust that the spectators at ground level had not seen half the race. Even after the horses disappeared, the residual hot winds of the Santana and the dust devils kept the dust in the air and continued to obscure the racing horses down San Pedro Street. Finally, the watchers who had climbed trees and onto the flat roofs of houses could see two horses returning, running through the crowds which partially blocked San Pedro Street. Finally, there was a small distinct circle of dust spiraling into the air, followed closely in its tail by a larger, less defined second spiral, caused by a horse running into the first dust cloud. Which horse had the lead?

Spectators on the tarred flat roofs of the adobe houses began shouting, although some cursed. Black Swan was leading! Now, Black Swan's jockey used his whip harder, drawing blood; Martinez, whipped Sarco constantly with his quirt as did his outriders, all drawing blood and Sarco began to inch up on Black Swan. Black Swan, with blood foaming from her mouth and nostrils, crossed the finish line barely a half-length in front of the gallant Sarco, who finished with bleeding flanks and a white froth foaming around mouth. Even Jose Martinez had received a whiplash across his neck in what was hopefully an errant whipping by an outrider. An initial hush swept over the crowd, perhaps in unconscious recognition of a new era, of the changes portended by the race. Some cried, some yelled, some beat on their friends.

Then a roar arose from the crowd of winners as if to announce, "The King is dead. Long live the King!"

I tromped dejectedly to the stables to see my friends, the Picos and the Carrillos. I knew they each lost a great fortune in the race and I wanted to console them. I hoped their Ranchos and families would survive intact. Before I reached them, Carlisle was at my left side.

"Counselor," he said, "Do you really know what happened?"

"No, and I don't want to know," I responded, fully aware this would goad Carlisle into a full explanation.

"We saw you secretly observing our training of Black Swan."

"I did not go there in secrecy, but went as anyone would. And yes, I did see the gentle training gradually increase to rigorous, hard training. I informed my other friends, the Sepulvedas and Carrillos about it. But they refused to change from their old ways.

"But tell me. Why was Black Swann's piss clear and odorless? I've never seen that before."

"We knew the weather would be hot and dry. Two days before the race, we began mild water loading her in anticipation she would need extra water in her blood, to cool her as she ran and perspired. She pissed so often, her passed water was colorless and odorless. We washed her muzzle and splashed her mouth before the race. Bill Brady wet her down as she left the barn and again at the turning post during the race, so that the evaporating water would cool her. We do the same to ourselves when it's hot. We take off our hats and douse our head in water.

"Using a professional jockey with the new type racing saddle just completed our business approach to the race."

As I walked away from him in disgust, I then knew the old society, which had united Alta California together under New Spain and then Mexico, was lost, that unacceptable changes were fast approaching, and that men such as Carlisle were the forerunners of the change. Honor was gone. Trickery, clothed in the guise of business was present. Winning was all, methods and friendship were secondary.

I wanted men to be honest in friendships and business. Our world was changing and I didn't like it.

# July 3, 1865; Assault on the Kingdom

It was at a very early daybreak that 3rd of July as I left my home, the Sanchez House, an adobe house outwardly clad with red brick walls and a Spanish tile roof. This elegant house was located on the short Sanchez Street running into the South side of the old Plaza, just around the corner from Pio Pico's adobe on the Plaza itself.

It was still darker than early morning; the weather was balmy with just a slight hint of an almost imagined briny breeze blowing on-shore from Santa Monica Bay, and I had a long way to go. The gentleness of the weather certainly did not portend the horror of the coming week that was to change my entire life.

I saddled up my gelding Frank, who did not live up to his name as he had hidden areas of uncommon behavior, most of which were good, but none of which were revealed. We turned left on the corner of Paseo de la Plaza and rode slowly west on the Plaza past the adobe of Jose Antonio Carillo, then ambled north on Main Street to Aliso Street, then down to the Los Angeles River which we forded just above the Zanja Madre where it drew its water at the junction with the low dam. Then on to the El Camino Real.

Increasing our pace on that grandly named path which was bordered by the occasional eucalyptus tree, Frank trotted north and east towards the Mission San Gabriel Arcangel. After we passed *The Locust*, a commodious adobe home built adjacent to the Mission by Laura's father, Alcade John R. Evertsen, I guided the reins over Frank's neck so they fell from right to left, gently touching only the right side of his neck. Obediently, Frank nosed his way left onto the poorly defined path of the Foothill Trail. Our goal was the Rancho Santa Ana del Chino, a long day's ride. Finally, Robert S. Carlisle was to receive his last and most enduring setback to his murderous career and I was the agent to deliver it to him.

"Frank," I said, "This time we have him. We almost had him for killing that nester years ago, but the jury, all ranchers, would have killed the nester too. So they let Carlisle go. But now, he tried to kill his sister-in-law and we finally obtained a confession from an accomplice. We got 'em."

Frank just trotted on, eyes focused upon the path ahead, ears twitching to my customary voice, calming him and allowing me to think out loud, without Frank even neighing a response.

The War of Northern Aggression had just concluded on April 9, both sides losing the best of their young men, with the Northern Army of Aggression driving helpless soldiers and families before them, destroying, plundering and raping their way to the shores of the Southern Seas. I wondered how long the enmity of war would last--much longer than our lives I mused. We in Southern California were probably very fortunate after California approved the bill to separate into two states which Governor John Weller signed in 1859, that the U.S. Congress killed it in fear of South California becoming a southern state aligned against the forming northern union.

We rode on, Frank following the trail without my guidance, while I mused and remembered the time I first heard of the battle of Bull Run, that glorious day in July of '61. Once again in memory, I stood upon the bar at the Bella Union Hotel and again pronounced, "We stand here today celebrating the first of our many victories, The Battle of Bull Run and Manassas. Our true patriotic feelings of our homeland are strong, as is our love for our families and homes there. We should rise against these few Union Republicans in our fair City of the Queen of the Angels, and march Eastward through the deserts to meet our men in uniform at Fort Yuma who are trying to free us from the Northern grasp, who after all, desire only the gold of California so as to destroy our southern heritage."

And soon thereafter, The Bella Union Hotel was declared off limits to all Union personnel. There had been too many fights between the southern political group and the Army of Northern Aggression. The U.S. Army even locked the doors of the Bella Union, the finest hotel in Los Angeles, for a few short days.

Again during the first part of July but in '62, almost on the anniversary of Bull Run, I stood once more on the stage of The Belle Union Hotel and repeated the toast. "Gentlemen, we are again gathered here to celebrate the Battle of Bull Run and Manassas and our victory there. But now, we can celebrate the victory of the Second Battle of Bull Run! But it seems as if, we too, must wage warfare against our own Northern brothers. Despite the fact that Abraham Lincoln received only 350 votes from Los Angeles in his election of 1860, and we Southerners cast 1,190 for his opponents, demonstrating our true relationship with our family and friends at our Southern homes, the Union has now established a US Army post at Camp Fitzgerald just adjacent to our Plaza, and is building another fort at Camp Drum in Wilmington. We must stop them from further action if we are to protect our homes in our fair City of our Queen of the Angels. California should be partitioned into two large sections, Southern and Northern California just as we voted to do in '59. This time we should not allow our former brothers from the North, an opportunity to again reject us from so doing by their manipulations in the United States Congress.

"Ah ha. Mr. Carlisle, I see you entering our Southern home, again uninvited. And pointing your extended arm and hand at me!

"And you bring a man with you; one who is certainly not a guest, but one whom we will arbitrarily chose to honor. Major James Henry Carleton. Pray sir, why do you honor us with your presence?"

"Honorable Assemblyman Andrew Jackson King, I am here to hold you for the United States Army, because of treason and preaching sedition, specifically because you cheered Jefferson Davis a month ago. If you give me your word, I shall not bind you but allow you to walk with me to our headquarters."

"I give you my pledge. But today is a sorry day for the history of our fair city, in which a military force usurps power from its elected, civilian leaders."

Looking back in retrospect from the protected year of July 1865, we in California were fortunate to lose so few volunteers and without confiscation of our property. After all, more than half of our citizens were from our southern states. Carlisle, a pretend southerner from Virginia but who was actually a powerful Union spokesman, had become wealthy, and profited from selling cattle to both sides during the war. He had seen to it that I, a duly qualified attorney at law, an Under Sheriff of Los Angeles City and County, and an Assemblyman of the State of California, had been arrested for preaching treason and sedition from the stage of the Bella Union Hotel way back in '62, and locked into the jail at Fort Los Angeles, then transferred to the military stockade at Drum Barracks, Wilmington.

I wonder if the Northern faction of the politicos had really believed me then when I promised I would no longer praise our southern brethren and swore an oath of allegiance to the Union. I was released after only two days imprisonment and as in hallowed times, allowed to go forth unto the land. Or were the toy boy soldiers, those failed gold minors, those Northern sympathizers in training at their Fort Drum Barracks, really concerned about the Los Angeles Rangers or The Monte Boys freeing me in a more dramatic way if I were not immediately released?

Actually, upon release I headed straight for the Bella Union Hotel, our de facto Southern headquarters and bought a round of drinks for all present to again celebrate our Southern victory at Bull Run, as I had done in '61. Later I learned my brothers Francis Marion and Samuel Houston heard about my imprisonment and were busily working with The Monte Boys and The Los Angeles Rangers to assault the military barracks and free me. But my quick release had stopped that plan and now, they just joined all the other well-wishers at the crowded Bella Union.

"But now, I've got Carlisle!" I exclaimed to Frank, who just twitched his ears and trotted on.

"We're riding on incredibly lush beautiful land, just waiting for crops and cattle. That Don Antonio Lugo certainly had huge cojones back in 1810 when he asked the King of Spain for this enormous Rancho of some 40,000 acres for military services rendered by his father, a simple soldier. Although I must admit, that walking for eight months from Sonora through the deserts of Baja to the Pueblo as a six year old child could not have been easy. This Rancho doesn't end until it becomes Rancho Cucamonga! Frank, would you have given up your cojones so easily if you could have had your pick of all the mares back then?"

I'll swear there was an immediate break in his stride as he lifted his leg to step over a fallen tree limb.

"Slow down my friend. There's the trail to Mud Springs. Rubottom's Tavern is right close and we don't want to pass by without lunch and a beer."

I watered Frank at the trough by the side of the tavern, loosened his cinch, settled the saddle and fed him some corn and oats and hitched him to the post under the huge oak. It wouldn't do well to have him unprepared for a long, perhaps hurried run so close to Carlisle's Rancho Cucamonga.

"Buenas tardes, Billy! I notice your tavern is almost empty today."

"Jack! Good to see you again. And this time, not in your official capacity I hope!"

"No, not at all. Just stopping for a bite and a beer."

"Jack, I've been thinkin'. Remember last year? Those cowboys who wanted to hang Merced? Everyone has always thought that those drunken cowboys in here were the Monte Boys. I don't think so. Why would they come here to drink themselves into hanging Merced? Why would they allow themselves to drink and yell themselves into a frenzy in a tavern next to her property where she would be known and protected? They had to have been strangers!

"Although the Monte boys may have hung a few innocents, those "innocents" were always guilty of other hanging crimes. And the boys always protected women. Why would the Monte Boys have wanted to hang Merced? I don't believe it. And besides, I would have recognized em if they had been Monte Boys.

"They were a bunch of drunken strangers."

"Billy, I'm certain they were Northern sympathizers who were drinking here that night in December of '62. They probably wanted Merced's entire property to go to Carlisle as the North needed the cattle for beef and hides. With Merced hanging and dead, Carlisle would have seen the remainder of her property pass directly to him through a paper purchase, or to his wife, Francisca, Merced's only legitimate sister.

"Perhaps you're unaware, but Merced's dead husband, John Rains, was a secret member of our *Knights of the Golden Circle* in El Monte, the inner circle of the Monte Boys. He may have been our compadre, but he was not an honest man. As soon as he married Merced, he stole her half of the Chino Rancho, really gifting her 24,000 acres to Carlisle for only 500 dollars! Rains then got title to the 17,000 acres of Rancho Cucamonga in his name only! And Merced didn't even find out about this until after his death!

"It was all high politics with tremendous stakes."

"I sure didn't know all that. My legs were shaking behind the bar; and I was afraid my voice would show it. But I couldn't let them drunken cowboys just up and hang a good woman. My shotgun was loaded, but it had only one shell in each barrel. If I had pulled the two triggers and then broke the gun open to reload, they sure would've got me."

"Billy, you're a true hero. You held those nine drunken cowboys off with just a shotgun, forced them to shuck their guns, and then to leave in pairs.

"Billy, this attempt to hang her actually began to play out a month earlier when her husband was killed by so-called, unknown parties. In mid-November, Rains left the Rancho on a business trip to Temecula on Monday. His two horses returned to the ranch without him on Wednesday. When businessmen from Los Angeles arrived on Friday asking for him, everyone was alerted that he was missing and Merced notified our Sheriff Tomas Sanchez."

"A.J., I know that.

"We raised a posse here at the tavern and began searching Saturday morning even before Sheriff Tomas Sanchez began searching from Los Angeles. We didn't find Rains' wagon until the next Tuesday, a week after he left for Los Angeles. It was in the bushes at Mud Springs just a little ways from here; the harness was in a tree and his bloody coat and hat were thrown on the ground. It wasn't until Friday of that second week that we found his dead body in a cactus patch even closer to my tavern. He had been lassoed by his right arm and dragged four hundred yards off the trail. Tore his arm right out of its socket. He was shot in the back twice, once in his chest, and once in his side. We brought his body back here and I laid him out on that big table until we found a wagon to take him back to the Rancho."

"Actually, the story doesn't end there, Billy."

"No?"

"There's a lot more to tell.

"This was in the middle of the war. And in Los Angeles, the Republican Party was in the saddle. Politically, they decided Californios Don Ramon Carrillo and Manuel Cerradel were in the group that murdered Rains. Luckily, our Court was strong and honest. Carrillo came to the Court voluntarily to be questioned for the offense, twice. Each time, the verdict was, 'The People of the State of California have no complaint against Ramon Carrillo and there is no reasonable cause to believe Carrillo guilty of the heinous crime of murdering John Rains.'

"Manuel Cerradel was actually tried for the murder of John Rains and the jury declared him 'Not guilty of the murder of John Rains'. But at the same trial, he was convicted of assaulting the Deputy Sheriff who had arrested him and he was sentenced to San Quentin. Tomas Sanchez and I, in our official capacity as Sheriff and Under Sheriff of Los Angeles, accompanied Cerradel on the tugboat *Cricket* from San Pedro Harbor to the coastal steamer *Senator* lying out in deep water, bound for San Francisco and San Quentin. Unbeknownst to us, the other passengers on the *Cricket* were vigilantes. They overpowered us and hung Cerradel from the yardarm. But before he died, he attested that Robert S. Carlisle was one of the murderers of Raines. And nothing ever happened to Carlisle!

"No official action was ever taken against Carlisle. He and his Republican friends were just too powerful. Carlisle claimed that he wasn't even in the County- that he was in San Bernardino that very same Monday, November 17th, to be sworn in as a newly elected member of the San Bernardino County Board of Supervisors. He claimed he could not have murdered Rains, his brother-in-law. But it was proven he did not appear at that board meeting in San Bernardino and he didn't present evidence of where he was on that fateful Monday! We all knew he was a member of the party that shot Rains. But we couldn't make the courts move against him.

"Billy, I'm tired and thirsty after talking so much. There is so much more to tell. Get us another mug of beer and we'll jaw on. You and your tavern are even more recently enmeshed in this saga about that poor widow. You must remember it well."

"Yeah, Jack. How could I forget? That murder was as brutal as the murder of Rains."

"Billy, you're speaking of the later attacks against Merced. First let me tell you more about the cause behind Raines' murder. This began about a year before the actual killing.

"John Rains married Merced when she was only 17, the very day after her father, Don Julian Williams died. You probably knew Don Julian as Colonel Isaac Williams who married Maria de Jesus Lugo, daughter of Antonio Maria Lugo. Her great grandfather was Francisco Salvador Lugo, a soldier who accompanied the Pobladores from Sonora through Baja to Alta California in 1781 and in turn, had been given the Spanish land grant of Rancho Santa Ana del Chino in 1841. Rains deliberately kept his wealthy bride inexperienced in business matters so he could steal her property.

"The day after Rains died, Merced learned that he had caused all of her property to be transferred to him. And then he upped and died without a will. She was penniless! She went to the court and was fortunate to have Benjamin Hayes as her judge.

"Hayes is our type of man; rode his mule from Missouri to our pueblo in 1850. By instinct, he went straight to the Bella Union and had a drink. Of course, it was the only hotel in town. Told everyone he was an attorney and became the first American lawyer to establish a practice here in Los Angeles.

"On March 12, 1863, Judge Hayes ruled that all properties were to be recorded in Merced's name. On March 13, the next day, the deeds were so recorded.

"But this didn't stop Carlisle. The very next day, March 14, 1863, he and five friends confronted her in her Cucamonga house. About four months after Rains was murdered, Merced, now 23 and a widowed mother of four, without formal education, inexperienced in business, and who barely understood some basic English, was confronted by six powerful political figures purporting to be her friends: her brother-in-law Robert S. Carlisle; the newly appointed administrator of the Cucamonga Estate Elijah K. Dunlap; three attorneys, James H. Lander, Jonathon R. Scott, and Alden A. M. Jackson; and her uncle who was a former Alcade and who later became Mayor of Los Angeles, Steven C. Foster.

"These six men, speaking only English, lied to her all day, claiming that Judge Hayes had recommended she give an irrevocable power of attorney to Carlisle, and transfer all her property to her children. Worn out after the long day, she signed the documents that were drawn up by the Harvard trained attorney, Lander and which were notarized by the attorney and notary, Jackson.

"Carlisle immediately purchased one half of the 17,000 acre Rancho Cucamonga estate for 300 dollars. The estate was looted of further monies when false claims of indebtedness were paid to three of the six figures who had forced Merced to sign the transfer of her property. No monies were provided to the estate for any reason and soon, the tax collector seized Merced's property because of non-payments. It was as if Carlisle wished to destroy the family so even their very existence would disappear. The Rains family had no food, no monies and no income. The Honorable Judge Hayes kept the family from actual starvation with gifts of food and supported them from his own meager means.

"After Hayes directly confronted this open abuse of power by Carlisle and the northern political establishment, it's not surprising that he, Judge Benjamin Ignatius Hayes, was defeated in his judicial reelection later that same year by Pablo de la Guerra, a moderate Californio attorney. But Billy, you must remember the Confederate Army was threatening Fort Yuma, and planning to proceed further west to the ocean and annex at least Southern California. The voters were perhaps correct in being fearful of a Southern sympathizer in any elected category.

"After the loss of his judgeship, Merced hired the former Judge Hayes as her attorney to recover her property. After all the attempts to steal her property, he was the only attorney she trusted. On February 13, 1864, Carlisle attempted to sell of all of her property but failed to complete the transactions. Less than two weeks later, on February 22nd, Hayes, representing Dona Maria Merced Williams du Rains, formally filed an action to recover all of her property by removing Carlisle from his power of attorney which had been obtained without consideration and by fraud, and revoking all of his actions over her property in San Bernardino, San Diego, and Los Angeles, including the vineyard of Cucamonga.

"Such legal notices would never stop Carlisle and he, once again, on April 9, purchased Merced's one-half interest in the extensive Rancho Valle de San Jose in San Diego for 300 dollars.

"And Billy, you and your tavern again saved Merced's life and her unborn child that same spring of '64. Remember in early May, Merced, now carrying her fifth child, screamed as she drove by your tavern, 'They killed him! They killed him! They shot him in the back!'

"While you and others were straddling your horses, her ranch foreman, Ramon Carrillo staggered and stumbled down the Foothill Trail, bleeding from his chest and spitting blood for the last thousand yards, collapsed in front of your tavern. You carried Ramon inside and placed him on the same big table where Merced's husband had been laid back in November of '62. Ramon gave a declaration as he was dying, 'Carlisle shot me in the back! His first shots missed, but when I turned in the saddle and looked backward, I saw him aim again and shoot me!' Merced was here by that time and she remembers that.

"Merced had been fearful for her life ever since she had filed her law suit against Carlisle in February, and had asked her foreman Carrillo to ride behind her buggy for protection. When the group of riders came up behind them, she heard the gun shots and whupped her horses to get away. She thought Ramon had been killed when he was shot off his horse and she would be next, for she was the one they wanted.

"It took another year for the courts to decide her claims against

Carlisle. In all that time, Carlisle had not been charged for the murder of Carrillo although the Mexican community was in an uproar. He was just too powerful in the Republican Power Community to be reached. But now, on May 15 of this year, 1865, Hayes was able to win the suit against Carlisle, and Judge Samuel McKee Bell ruled against Carlisle. Carlisle no longer controls her estate and must disgorge all of his misbegotten spoils! And I, Under Sheriff and former Assemblyman, newspaper publisher and attorney, have been appointed as receiver to manage her property! The Court has finally taken judicial notice of the criminal behavior of Carlisle even though they have not noticed his murdering ways. We did have him examined for the killing of John Rains, with a witness and all. But vigilantes, probably Carlisle's friends, hanged that witness against Carlisle from the yardarm of The Cricket. And Carlisle again escaped his due justice. But now, we're taking the first step to bring him down. Too bad we can't just throw a rope over the branch of an oak and take care of the problem in our old fashion way.

"I'm on my way to Chino to serve Court Papers on him. I was appointed as the receiver of all of Merced's property from here to San Diego. Carlisle has lost control of her properties! This will really cause an explosion. I wonder what he'll do?"

"Jack, do you believe you can go there alone? Carlisle has hard men with him at all times. They draw his pay and will be loyal to his brand."

"No. I think it's better without a posse. From my experience, someone in a posse always starts shooting. I'm not taking him in. Just letting him know I'm taking charge. There isn't much left anyway. He's been selling everything off for longer than two years despite the court ruling. Perhaps he'll be tried later and sentenced to San Quentin. He really belongs there, along with some others we can name.

"Thanks again. Frank and I will be on our way now. Adios."

And again, we trotted off in the midday heat, eastwards on the Foothill Trail.

The days were still long, this 3rd of July and shadows were stretched and grotesque as we approached Carlisle's house on the Rancho Santa Ana del Chino. The high sun was at my back, my face masked in my own shadow. It was no longer morning, but was the beginning of later afternoon following a long day's ride. I carefully kept my hands in clear view, away from my side, showing no gun, holding only my reins. Perhaps this is why I was allowed so close to the Hacienda before Breed, with a half dozen vaqueros at his side, yelled, "Stop!"

His men immediately fanned out, their eyes squinting into the sun, peering from a wide arc toward me. They could see no other man on the trail, which did not reduce the tension as someone could be hiding in the scrub to the side. "Breed," I yelled, "I must see Carlisle and talk to him."

"No, you won't. The Don told me not to let you through. Turn around and go back whole."

I heard the click of six hammers being drawn back on their pistols; hopefully there would be no loose pin where the hammer would slip and the gun would fire. If one shot were fired through carelessness, all would fire in the tenseness of the confrontation. A moment later, there was the metallic clack of the slide of a lever-action rifle loading a cartridge into the chamber, then another clack from across the path. They were all around me! How many gunslingers did Carlisle have? They were in front of me, and on both sides; and did I hear the movement of horses behind me as well? And those repeating rifles were 15 shots each. One man and a horse could do nothing against these fighting men. This was a new experience to me, facing so many gunmen alone; so different than when I had faced the killer of my father, mano a mano.

"I need to deliver some court papers to him. They're in my bag here. I'll throw it to you and you can take it to Carlisle."

"Don't move! Don't make a move with your right hand! Drop your bag at your side. Then git! I'll take it to the Don. Do it now or you'll be planted where you stand."

I dropped the bag with my left hand, holding both reins in my right. Then I slowly changed the position of my left hand, reached and grasped the left of the split reins with my left hand, and gently pulled back both reins steadily and slowly backed off Frank, always looking at Breed, never challenging him or his vaqueros by sign or movement. At fifty feet distance, I slowly turned Frank, then spurred him to a fast start, weaving from side to side. As anticipated, pistol shots were fired at me but all missed our bobbing, moving figures, blurred in the halo of the low lying sun. Fortunately there were no booms of the more accurate, heavy rifle shots. Were they just firing at me to make me dance? Or to make me nervous and defeated? If they had really wanted me dead, they could have killed me at any time. This was a lot different than when I faced only one gunslinger.

Delivery of the documents had been accomplished and no one was shot. A good beginning had been made for the end game to be fought in the courts. But should I have come alone? Why did I choose to do it that way?

The further we trotted from the Rancho, the more relaxed I became. Although I would admit it to none, I later even slept a little on the long ride home. Frank was a very wise horse and knew his way home to the Plaza and Sanchez Street without my guidance. Once home, Laura would be able to sleep soundly, although I would lay awake beside her for a long time, sometimes trembling.

# July 5, 1865; Attempted Murder

The day awakened with a rooster's early cry at the beginning of the false dawn when the cotillion of stars were slowly dancing their way into darkness, accompanied by a falling moon in the West, chased by a glowing red dawn in the East.

The streets of old Los Angeles, even Main Street, were filled with offal and other aromatic rubbish daily, thrown aside by the local inhabitants after slaughtering their food in their front yards. Scavengers fought one another for these remains, leaving but a few inedible inorganic detritus, but little could be done about the constant smell of death and rotting remains.

There were no provisions to clean the streets of Los Angeles except to remove dead bodies, for they were unsightly and with an all too distasteful sweet human cadaver smell. An exception was made for Fiesta Days when in the early mornings, cleansing began. This was equally true on that Tuesday Fourth of July of 1865, when the streets were swept in honor of that new National Holiday in our new State of California.

Main Street of old Los Angeles and the Central Plaza were swept again that early Wednesday morning, the morning following the raucous Fourth of July celebration. This time, only five bodies were found on the streets; as usual, Indians and Orientals were not counted. One of those dead proved to be only dead drunk, and he scared the sweepers when he yelled at monsters only he could see and then began his ritualistic shakes. After the bodies were removed and the cow pies and horse apples had been swept aside, the dust was dampened with water from the Zanja Madre and stomped hard, for one of the most important social events of the year was to begin at four o'clock that afternoon.

It was to contrast sharply with the despair felt by most Angelinos, for the drought was upon Southern California as a biblical plague of yore. Times had changed and cattle could not be sold. There was no demand for meat with the overnight disappearance of the '49er market. They even were not worth slaughtering for their hides; the California Dollar had vanished with the depression. Ranchos and ranches were in foreclosure, as the ruinous interest of up to 12% monthly on land debts could not be paid; many land titles fell to the city and county when owners could not even pay their land taxes. Sheriff Sanchez held even Abel Stern's property through civil actions, and Abel Sterns was still the richest man in California. The jails were filled with the poor and those who had no monies and who had turned to petty crimes in order to eat.

That Wednesday afternoon of July 5, 1865, the misery of the poor and hungry of Los Angeles contrasted with the opulence of the wedding ceremony of Miss Caroline, third daughter of wealthy Joseph Newmark, who wed Mr. Solomon Lazard of the even wealthier and politically stronger Lazard family. It was an occasion for the society elite of Los Angeles, quiet and distinguished, pleasant and above all, happy and joyous.

Preparation for the wedding had begun months earlier. Invitations printed on a pink Bristol board were delivered to the homes of a selected two hundred of the Ton. Tensions were high inside the grand homes of Los Angeles as the all-white carriage drawn by two white horses appeared on the street. Gentle ladies were relieved when the carriage halted at the path to their door and the footman delivered invitations touched only with white gloves. All those invited, attended.

I didn't understand why Laura was so anxiously waiting for an invitation. She stood by our upstairs window, looking cornerwise out to the Plaza for the white carriage to appear, and when it did, she rushed down stairs, almost tripping on the narrow 13th tread, to sit calmly (or at least to appear so) in a chair and pick up a book to "read."

"Laura," I said, "Don't worry. My standing in society will ensure that we receive an invitation. And then, I am in several business ventures with Lazard, including forming the new Los Angeles Water Company. Lazard cannot afford to forget that and he is, above all, an astute business man."

"AJ, you just don't understand, do you. To you, this is just business. But if we don't receive an invitation, and Dad does, and I'm certain he will, it will be another mark he'll hold against you, another reason we should not have married."

"Laura, the coach is stopping in front of our house, the Sanchez House, one of the finest homes on the Plaza, one of the few with a tile roof, built when our Pueblo was under the rule of Spain, through Felipe de Neve, their Viceroy of New Spain. And the messenger and his white gloves are now walking to our door. Relax and greet him as you would. Or should I accept the invitation from him? Perhaps you would want Maria to answer the door and request that he await your pleasure?"

Laura was correct and she and I were envied as it became known that we had received a wedding invitation and an invitation to the wedding banquet later in the evening. To my surprise, even my friends whom I met during the next few working days were aware of the invitations and remarked on them.

The wedding ceremony actually began on the Shabbat, the Saturday of July 1, before the wedding day. The groom and the bride were called to the Torah in an aufruf during the special service for them, reciting the blessings before and after the reading of the Torah. There were few congregants as there were but a few Jews in Los Angeles but those present, sang a song in the couple's honor.

The wedding was solemnized four days later in the mid afternoon at the Main Street home of Maurice Kremer, Miss Caroline's brother-in-law.

The wedding guests began to arrive at 3 o'clock. Laura and I were cordially greeted by the parents of the bride and the groom, and shown to a hat and cloak apartment where guests were relieved of their outer vestments. We were then escorted down the short hall to the parlors that had been thrown open to make one huge room, allowing the compliment of guests to mingle without crowding.

I believed the couple were married during the ceremony on Saturday, five days earlier, and was astounded when the wedding ceremony began as the bride and groom were escorted down the aisle between the guests by their parents. At this point in the ceremony, Laura began to describe the meaning of the ceremony to me. I just stared at her as she whispered.

"Laura? Where did you learn this?"

"Jack, you were so busy serving your warrants, you didn't even notice I was gone during the day, busy visiting Caroline. I assisted them as a good friend would and learned the meaning of the beautiful ceremony."

The bride and groom separated from their parents as they went under the wedding canopy, the huppah. The bride's father hurried around the huppah and approached it from the rear. Mr. Joseph Newmark was the lay rabbi of Los Angeles, and served two functions during this particular wedding, as the father of the bride and as the Rabbi conducting the ceremony.

A glass of wine was handed to Rabbi Newmark and he recited a blessing over it. The bride and the groom sipped the wine. The couple then exchanged rings of solid gold as they solemnly recited an ancient vow, "By this ring you are consecrated to me according to the Law of Moses and Israel."

Rabbi Newmark then read the Ketubah.

Laura whispered an explanation to me. "This is a written Jewish marriage contract, originally written in Aramaic more than 2,000 years ago, the language of ancient Babylon and recited in Jewish marriage ceremonies ever since. But our lay Rabbi does not know the language of the ancient Jews and uses modern Hebrew in his reading to the congregation.

"The Ketubah states the names of the married couple and the date and place of the wedding. It describes the spiritual commitment to one another and there is an exchange of promises to care for one another and to make a Jewish home. It passes on Jewish customs from one generation to the next; it creates a new family.

"The wedding canopy, the huppah, is important in their tradition. It is a symbol of the past, of thousands of years ago, of the tent in the desert where the newly married couple spent their wedding night. But it is also the symbol of the future, of the Jewish home that the couple will build together. "Tears were flowing from her eyes as she whispered to me, and then I accepted the meaning and tradition which is so lacking in our brief sterile ceremonies, which are almost limited to only the signing of the wedding contract and self-serving statements of itinerant preachers.

The bride wore a white silk dress and later, Laura informed me that the canopy of the huppah was of the same fine material, hung over four corner poles as if it were an ethereal tent. One could not see the wood of the poles as vines of our California region circled them, and blossoms covered all areas, twisting and turning their way up to the heavens.

Following the Ketubah, Rabbi Newmark chanted the Seven Blessings, thanking God for creating the universe, people and wine. The Seventh Blessing asks God to bring joy and happiness to the new couple. The couple then drank the wine and Rabbi Newmark declared them married under the Jewish law and the law of the State of California.

I couldn't believe my eyes but I swear this is what happened next. "I saw the Rabbi wrap the empty glass with a cloth, place the cloth on the floor, and then, the groom crush the glass with his foot. Then all the celebrants shout, 'Mazal Tov'.

"The wedding ceremony was now complete and the chairs were moved to the walls of the room. Suddenly, the Temple was a celebratory room.

"The bride and groom danced around one another in a ritualistic movement, not touching but joined with a white cloth which each grasped at a corner. Next, their friends and family placed the bride and groom onto chairs, lifted the chairs on their shoulders and danced around the room in joy. These leaders of Los Angeles, respected and staid, celebrated and danced for the next hour as if they were but young, carefree men with their best girls. I just don't understand them." I knew it was this long for I clocked it with my golden watch that was always with me in my vest pocket.

The dresses of other ladies were conservative, but certainly functional and did not prohibit their dancing following the ceremony. My attire was similar to other Anglos; we wore our finest business suits; most of us saved our formal clothing for the evening banquet and the grande fete at the Bella Union Hotel.

Suddenly, I noticed that arrogant, insolent criminal Carlisle was there with his wife Francisca, impeccably attired as always; he in formal black with a black tie, and she, the innocent, in a Californios costume as benefited her station as the daughter of a Spanish land grantee, descendant of those who walked the long journey from Sonora, New Spain to the El Pueblo de la Reyna de Los Angeles, protecting the Pobladores. I wondered how Carlisle could appear so calm in public view, just the day after I had served him with writs that were really criminal indictments.

Carlisle was a large man, more than six feet in height, with a deep booming voice. He used these physical attributes to project an extraordinary presence of gregariousness and magnanimity, as assured as if he were King George at his court, with all present as loyal courtiers. How could this magnificent presence be so criminal in nature? Did he not notice me or did he just deign not to recognize his adversary? Were his minions awaiting my appearance outside, to attack me there? Somehow, the whole world appeared upside down, where the bad were up, and the good and the innocent were down.

Many Californios wore more splendid attire to the wedding then did the Anglos, with red silk lined black capes allowing them to display their former Spanish and Mexican uniforms and decorations as if sitting for a portrait, with an occasional ceremonial sword projecting through the frame. Their women were just as formal, but saved their more traditional dresses for the grande fete.

These caballeros would not condescend to walk down Main Street and cross the Plaza on foot. Following the ceremony, they mounted their gallant silver and gold clad horses and pranced a few feet around and by the Plaza to the Bella Union Hotel, the finest hotel in Los Angeles since its dedication in 1849. The building even had served briefly as the capital of California in 1846. The ladies and family rode more sedately in carriages, some even in shaded ox drawn carretas, to their town houses where they rested for the evening dinner and the dancing.

The wedding party was to begin at 8 1-2 o'clock with a sumptuous repast, to be followed by a Fandango. It was the talk of the town for weeks, as the banquet was promised to be of Lucullan prominence although this time, Lucullus would not sup only with Lucullus.

Following the conclusion of the four o'clock wedding, Laura and I returned to our home on Sanchez Street, on the opposite side of the Plaza from the Kremer's home. I then walked around the corner to where my friends were waiting for me at the ground floor bar of the Bella Union Hotel, just south of The Plaza at 314 North Main Street.

In the early evening shadows, we could see the edge of the crowd on the Paseo. The hotel had constructed a raised brick walk in front of it on Main Street back in '54, and when the hotel tore down its adobe walls and refaced them with brick walls in '61, the hotel was a perfectly matched, three story building. They also laid an elegant flagstone over the dirt floor of the bar. This resulted in the most impressive building in Los Angeles, it looked as if it were really the present capitol of California, and looked far grander than when it was the capitol building for a month or so back in 1845. A young magnolia tree planted in a wooden container placed just outside the doorway stretched its branches high so that a tall man could walk under them without removing his hat.

Judge Benjamin Hayes and the outstanding attorney William C. Dryden had selected a quiet table in the back of the room and I joined them. Mr. Mario di Tullio, an Italian grape grower and wine maker, joined us later in discussing the new cash crop, walnuts, which were planted in large acreage at Lexington and the Willows, now named El Monte. Our behavior and language was as sedate as our formal attire but became more serious when I began discussing the service of warrants on Carlisle yesterday.

The group at a table across the room from us, was not so mannered; their voices were loud and frequently argumentative, the gestures overly dramatic and as uncontrolled as their imbibing of liquor. Carlisle was at that table without his family. Although he had appeared sober at the wedding, his reputation by now was of an individual described as obnoxious when sober, and volatile, explosive and just plain mean when drinking. It soon became apparent he had been drinking in the bar the entire afternoon following the wedding and he was the most vociferous of his group. As soon as the liquor in him reached the level of his mouth, he began to heckle me.

"Hey there, Sheriff! You couldn't even find me yesterday could you? What's the matter? Scared off by shadows? Can't ride in the dark without losing your way? Probably afraid to carry a gun! Just keep out of my path and you'll live longer."

I had already told our table of the problems in serving the writs on Carlisle and of the wild shots fired at me. Again the question arose as to how politically strong Carlisle stood in our Los Angeles, for no one even suggested that he be arrested for the behavior of his men. Legally, I could understand that, for we didn't arrest a man for merely shooting at another, but only if a man were seriously injured in an unfair fight. Still, someone was responsible for his men shooting at me, as I was an under-sheriff on official duty.

Judge Hayes, years ago had been a fearless man who rode his circuit alone, with only his guns to protect him. But since an assignation attempt in '51 along with his advancing age, the Judge was now a somewhat timid man. He had been the attorney for John Rains, Carlisle's brother-in-law whom Carlisle hated and who had been murdered two years previously under mysterious circumstances in which Carlisle had played a direct role.

Presently, Judge Hayes was the attorney for Merced Rains in the adjudication of her father's estate, contesting and confronting Carlisle, a documented killer, almost daily in Court. There was good reason to be concerned about Carlisle, especially now that he appeared to be losing everything. And Judge Hayes was probably fearful that Carlisle had seen him with me tonight.

Judge Hayes stood and stated, "Please excuse me. I'm tired. There will be trouble with Carlisle and I do not wish to be singled out by him. I survived one assassination attempt of his in November of '51 and next time, I may not be so fortunate. I'll go in to the wedding dinner with my wife, Emile, and then go home."

I responded for our table. "Please do so. If you like, we could escort you outside. Even an intoxicated Carlisle would not attempt to force his will upon all of us."

"Thank you, no. I'm certain he will have enough self-control in this crowd."

As dinner was announced, we also rose and proceeded up the gently curving stairs to the banquet room, pleased to note that the vociferous table remained behind. As we did, we heard a disturbance at the Main Street door to the bar, followed later by a gun shot in the street.

During dinner, I was told it was my brother, Francis Marion King, Deputy to Sheriff Tomas Sanchez, who wanted to join us in the hotel, walking through the bar. He was advised by friends not to enter, as it would provoke Carlisle to cause more unpleasantness during the wedding festivities.

Even outside the door, he could hear Carlisle comparing him and his brothers to certain indelicate animals, but he could not see inside the bar, where Carlisle was waving a Bowie knife to emphasize his intentions towards we three King brothers. Out of consideration for his friends and the wedding ball, gentle Francis walked away, alone, into the warm dark night.

I was informed later, that 29 year old Deputy Marshall John R. Evertsen, Jr. heard a pistol shot in the night and investigated the bar as a possible source. He heard Carlisle screaming threats against the Kings, but in the loud drunken crowd, he did not notice Carlisle's Bowie knife. He placed his hand on Carlisle's shoulder and announced, "Mr. Carlisle, I arrest you!"

"By whose authority?" retorted Carlisle angrily, pulling away from Evertsen, turning around and then pointing his Bowie at him.

"As an officer of the City of Los Angeles!"

Hearing this, Carlisle stabbed at Evertsen, who then noticed the 15 inch knife for the first time. He simply stepped back and the blade fell short. Dr. Winston yelled, "John, step back, get out the door. We'll take care of him now. Come back in the morning and arrest him then, when he's sober."

"OK. I don't want to shoot Carlisle just in order to arrest him. But watch out for him-my sister is married to A.J. and he hates A.J.

"I'll come back tomorrow morning with a warrant from the Court. It's better that way."

When I heard about this later after dinner, I was astounded that he had not been immediately arrested. But no one had been hurt and there was never a shortage of fighting drunks in the bars and streets of the City of the Angeles, which was often truly spoken of as the City of El Diablo.

Upstairs, the wedding banquet began promptly at 8 1-2 o'clock. It truly embraced "all the good things of earth." The chef was the personal chef of the French Consul, who was also present; but how did he prepare the Lucullan banquet for 100 guests? It was a ten-course dinner and beginning after the Soupe a L'oignon, each course was followed by different sorbets to cleanse the pallet.

The individual dishes were of local game and produce. Despite both members of the wedding couple being Jewish, oysters, mussels and all types of local shellfish, razor, pismo and butter clams, packed in barrels of ice along with abalone, and large limpets of unknown names, even giant crabs, lobster, octopus and squid were transported from San Pedro. Surf and deep-sea fish were packed in ice, but in different wagons.

The following courses were of venison, goats, small game of all types, and beef of all cuts and art of cooking, chicken and turkey. There was an inexhaustible supply of local game birds and ducks. A cornucopia of vegetables from the Los Angeles area proved our valley is a veritable Garden of Eden.

The dinnerware and flatware services were naturally French, but the glassware was thin stemmed Venicean goblets, so delicate several snapped during the evening, most of them at the close of the dinner following the many toasts. Many families must have contributed their services to provide place settings for a hundred diners.

The wines were excellent, both red and white, and again, were local, some from my families' vineyards in El Monte.

The attire of the men, white fronts on black, with an occasional star-like brilliant medal, were formal, almost a military guard, and were complementary to the glorious gowns of our ladies in all their delightful colors, presenting a bouquet of soft delicate flowers alternating with a stern line of attentive men. Behind each diner were two servers, and they too, were dressed in white tie.

The Californios blazed forth in all their glory with silken capes and golden swords encrusted with precious jewels, documenting that their Spanish empire was not waning although both Spain and Mexico had been dispossessed of Alta California. Their ladies were in scandalous deep decollate, bosoms protected with emerald, ruby and diamond necklaces from their former vast Asian Empires. Their younger ladies wore lustrous pearls from South Seas holdings, enhancing the youthful beauty of their glowing skin.

The orchestra, on a raised dais, played softly throughout the dinner. As the dessert of baked Alaska was concluded, we gentlemen retreated to the upstairs bar. The double mahogany doors were now closed and screened the bar from the dining room, so we could retire and smoke our cigars by an opened window while enjoying a postprandial brandy. We discovered to our delight that Mr. De Tullio had presented us a pipe of 20 year tawny port and many chose that delight.

The dining tables were cleared and removed; the orchestra played light melodies, and we stepped to the floor to observe the bride and groom begin their first dance as marriage partners. The men whose ladies were waiting for them, left the smoking room to begin the wedding Ball and later Fandango. I was pleased to dance with my beautiful wife, Laura. She remained at the Fandango with friends while I again retreated to a table at the second floor bar with my political friends.

Enjoying a snifter of tawny port, we sat silently, contemplatively. From a distance, we heard the voices of the young men and women, especially the cries of excitement and pleasure which came through the closed doors whenever a gentlemen broke a Cascarones or egg shell filled with small pieces of golden gilt or colored paper over the head of his dancing companion, paying her a wonderful compliment, and filling the immediate area with brilliant, glistening particles and light, wafting scents.

I wondered aloud, saying, "We're sitting here on the third floor of

La Bella Union Hotel, the highest building, the greatest hotel in Los
Angeles. This hotel is even grander than our La Iglesia de La Reina de
Los Angeles now that we have a stone floor on the ground. Our fair city
has progressed so much that the original adobe walls were taken out and
brick walls were substituted four years ago. Perhaps they should have
replaced the walls earlier when they added the brick sidewalk on Main
Street in 1854. I know the adobe walls of Colonel Williams old store here
with the outside sleeping screens upstairs, ran with thick mud every time
it rained. Yes, I know it is progress but it took an earthquake to make it
happen.

"Just 15 years ago, we came from Georgia to Sante Fe, then drove our
wagons and cattle for two months over the Old Indian Trail to reach El
Monte when Dad was wagon master. I can truly say there is no building
from Georgia, through Texas and New Mexico to rival our La Bella
Union."

Mr. Mario di Tullio, a master musician and now a grower of grapes
for fine wines, interrupted, "Excuse me, please. I have seen marvels of
the world of which you cannot even begin to dream. Here, let us fill our
glasses once again of this tawny port and I will tell you of the days when
Gods strode over our Roman homeland and built their earthly abodes
which still stand.

"Ah, is it not a great wine? Look at the deep red color, so clear that
one can see to infinity in its depths. Nectar of the Gods who are now
sharing it with us. Look into their wine and let me tell you of their stories.

"I say Gods, for when my parents in the old country took us on
family outings, we often drove our carriages to the Janiculum, a hill
outside Rome. In the early morning, one could look east, down across
the River Tiber and see the towers of an ancient city, spiking their tops
through the early morning mists-the ancient city of Rome showing above
the modern. In those early days, following Romulus and Remus suckling
their existence from the mother She-wolf, ancient Gods of bygone days
strode the earth and ruled all below.

"Just across the River Tiber, we saw the round tower of the
Pantheon-a temple built three centuries before our Lord walked the
earth, whose central room was round and dedicated to Gaea, the Earth

Goddess. It was so large, our Pueblo Plaza could fit into it, and we could walk around the Plaza without touching the inside walls of the Pantheon. There was but one narrow entrance and there were no windows.

"The first time Gaea entered her earthly abode above ground, the Demons of the Underworld gathered there had to flee. But they could not - there was neither an exit nor a second entrance. The Demons flew round and round, then broke a round hole in the roof and bolted into the sky.

"I, myself, have stood in that consecrated temple and looked straight up at that round hole in the sky. I basked in the light shining down at me, warming me, while I saw rain glistening in the sky over the Temple. Although I am a firm believer in our Christos, and I now cross myself twice to show you this, that day I felt Gaea was protecting me in her mantel of Earth and Sun. She and her other lesser Gods were beside me, holding that great dome up, high in the clouds of the sky, six times higher than this hotel. And there were no supporting walls!"

"Mister di Tullio, you speak of times I cannot comprehend and of fairy buildings I cannot even imagine. I speak of our times of today, not of hoary aged beings, but of the brutality of man who exerts himself to achieve more at the cost of those who cannot protect themselves. When our La Bella Union Hotel was rebuilt, the earthen floor yielded clay bowls and plates, woven baskets and wooden instruments that had been cast aside. Some say the Yang-na left them when they moved on to new dwellings. Laura describes the few pieces we collected for our home, as mysteriously beautiful, and we must save them for our lineage. She says the Yang-na had their cities along the river for thousands of years and more; I see only drunken bodies who are thrown into the cattle corral every Saturday or Sunday evening, and then sold as slaves for one week of indentured work, only to repeat the drunken cycle the next weekend. Where is their nobility? They are no ancient God figures! Where is their city with towers to the sky?

"Their degradation lies within themselves. Every year there are fewer of them; soon there will be none.

"But gentlemen, I apologize for my tirade. I cannot speak as to how the colonizers of Los Angeles treated their innocents. Slavery is bound to mankind; our hosts tonight built the pyramids and the sphinx of ancient Egypt before Moses lead them to their promised land. The Romans had their Greek and Christian slaves and when they invaded Britain, they found my ancestors living in trees and painting themselves with blue clay. 'In vino veritas', so I cannot apologize for the truth, but I do seek your understanding of my imbibition this evening.

"Sometimes I am Atlas, and the world becomes too heavy."

But this evening of joy and innocence abruptly came to a closure. An extremely loud but slurred voice rose from the nether regions of the hotel and floated up the stairs and above the ballroom, into our drawing room. "I'll get him! Where is he? I know he's here. Arrest me? I'll kill him as I did the others!"

And there was that Carlisle again, or at least his cry of anger. He had drunk his dinner, which was not good in a man with such limited control over his actions. He was unable to be reticent regarding my failed attempt to serve him a writ of attachment and theft of property. He certainly should not disturb such an elegant wedding party with such inappropriate behavior. It would also have been wiser to allow direct service of the warrants rather then having his armed vaqueros bodily eject me from his Cucamonga Rancho yesterday.

"If you'll please excuse me gentlemen, I'll leave before Mr. Carlisle becomes more agitated. His friends can scarcely contain him. Dryden, please accompany Laura outside where I'll wait for her. We'll meet early in the morning to discuss him further."

And I left, crossing the ballroom floor to the broad, curving staircase.

I descended perhaps half a dozen steps when inarticulate howls of anger blocked out all other sounds except the screams of Laura. I turned slightly to my left searching for her as Carlisle rushed up the stairs at me, screaming, "Jack King is a God dammed son of an ass!"

He slapped me on my left side-Now I knew why he always did this! He discovered that tonight I was not wearing my Dragoon in my shoulder harness!

I slapped Carlisle in the face with my open hand, hoping to bring awareness of the situation to his drunken mind. It proved to be meaningless. He continued his threats, then drew and brandished his 20-inch Bowie knife. "You! I'm going to kill you-carve you up! And I'm going to kill your brothers too, as soon as I see them!

"Tomorrow - noon at the Bella Union Hotel. I'll kill all of you."

"Jack!"- I could clearly hear Laura's warning cry, but I could do nothing.

Carlisle slashed and stabbed at my heart but in so doing, stumbled and fell a step or two lower, cutting only my jacket. Although tall, he now had to stab upwards, still missing me and cutting only my trousers. I leaned back, away from him, holding onto the curved banister for balance with my right hand. This turned me further to the left. He jumped forward and up, and stabbed again. Instead of skewering my heart, his Bowie blade hit my gold watch in the vest pocket, skipped across my watch chain crossing my waistcoat, stabbed, sliced and cut my stomach muscles, and ended stuck into my left arm. He twisted and pulled the knife free. Blood gushed as I fell; my white front turned scarlet, the black jacket shiny and even darker. The soft lamplight shone on the stairs that now glistened dark red. Even as I fell and hit the stairs, I reached into my right coat pocket, grasped the derringer hidee there and fired two shots through my jacket. The bullets did not hit him, but the close shots stopped a further attack.

Carlisle turned, ran down the stairs and through rowdy ground floor bar where his friends and vaqueros were drinking and partying.

My thoughts had been so focused upon saving my life that it was only then I heard the screaming of women and the yelling of the crowd. "Stop him!" screamed some, whilst others cried, "Get a doctor! --He's out the door!"

Losing consciousness fast, I could only whisper to the gathering crowd, "Send for Dr. Mayes. Warn my brothers Sam and Frank that they are next! That Carlisle said he would kill them! Kill us all! Carlisle can't be trusted! He's a dirty killer!"

I could not further speak but heard cries and screams. I felt soft but strong arms around me; my last fading vision was of my angel Laura holding me, her bodice and décolleté crimson red.

# July 6, 1865; Duel at the Bella Union Hotel

I awoke with sunlight shining in my eyes. It hurt when I tried to turn to my left where I had been stabbed, but I could turn my head to the right without too much pain. I then saw my brother-in-law, Dr. Alexander Mayes sitting at my bedside. "Where am I? What time is it?"

"You're at the Lafayette Hotel, across the street from the Bella Union. It's Thursday morning. How are you feeling?"

"I'm alive."

"And that's a surprise to all of us!" Laura added. "If Dr. Griffen had not been at the wedding party to staunch your bleeding, you would have died. He saved your life!"

Now, I slowly turned my head to the left, and found she was holding my left hand that poked out from all the wrapped linen. I just couldn't feel her hand. Nor could I really move any part of my body.

Laura continued. "Cousin Alex came by later last night, cleaned your wounds and poured alcohol over the slashes, which did not penetrate your belly. Carlisle only cut some muscles there which Alex sewed up."

"I can't even move my arm!"

"You'll be unable to use it for a while. It was cut deep. I sewed it together and wrapped it," Alex explained.

"But where is Carlisle? This madman must be stopped.

"We can't allow his threats to go unchallenged. Our lives would be worthless. Any dog in town would attack us without barking".

Laura responded, answering me in a soothing voice. "Jack, you have friends and family here. Look around. All have helped."

Alex continued. "Yes, we know about the threats. Francis Marion spoke earlier with Lander, that Texas lawyer friend of Carlisle's. Carlisle is in the Bella Union bar waiting for us. He's been drinking and scheming all night. He wants a shootout - threatens to kill all Kings on sight, even our women folk. I guess I fall in there too."

"The plan is to have our say with him just before noon. Carlisle wants to take the Banning Stage that will be loading just outside the Bella Union at noon. It's Steamer Day and The Senator will be sailing for San Francisco. There'll be a crowd waiting and Carlisle wants to climb aboard the stage when no one is watching and escape. The stage will take him to San Pedro Bay where he'll slip aboard the tow boat for The Senator and sail to San Francisco.

"It appears as if he is making a lot of plans for something which may not happen."

"What time is it?" I asked. And then I saw my golden time piece on the bureau, scratched, dented and discolored by dark red in the scratches. But it had saved my life and I knew that if I lived, I would have it reworked.

"It's ten and a half now."

"Alex, help me dress. I'm the best shot of the family. I'm the cause of the fight. I'm the one Carlisle truly wants to kill. He tried to kill me last night but couldn't bring it off. I must help Sam and Francis. I know Carlisle and he won't come alone. He'll bring Breed who has killed at least ten men and that Lander, a gunslinger from Texas but who claims to be a Harvard lawyer. He'll have his vaqueros hidden there in the bar as well. And every friend he has. I know him. He wants to wipe out all of us Kings, women and children as well!

"I'll need both pistols loaded, my old Dragoon horse pistol and my new Navy Colt, even though I can use only my right hand. Pull the bandage tighter so I can stand straight and walk. Help me up and get me dressed."

"Don't do it!" yelled Laura. "He can't even stand! We've been giving him whiskey and Laudanum all night. I don't know how he can even talk."

I attempted to sit up, but became dizzy, and fell back flat onto the bed, unconscious.


At first I heard the distant ringing of a huge sonorous resonating bell, then voices that gradually became clearer as the tones of the bell receded. "Carlisle…"

"Of course…"

Finally I heard a recognizable voice- Samuel continued speaking to me as if we had been talking with one another for some time. "A.J., you're supposed to stay in bed. Alex told us it would be a week before he would let you up."

"What are you and Francis doing here? And why is Laura here? I'm not dying am I? Where is Alex?"

"I drove in from the ranch this morning with a wagon load of lumber and barley, stopped off at the Sheriff's office to see you and Francis, and found Francis waiting for me. Everyone is talking about you being stabbed and killed, and that Carlisle has bragged that he would also kill all of us on sight.

Then the jailor, Henderson, walked in and said you weren't hurt as badly as was being told. We couldn't believe him and we had to come and see you ourselves."

"As you can see, I'm doing well. It's not as bad as it looks. I was just given too much Laudanum last night."

Francis Marion interrupted. "After we left the Sheriff's Office, Henderson ran to the Court House to tell Sheriff Sanchez that we were here. Sanchez ran down and saw me in Lazard's store when I was buying a segar. He asked me about you being knifed last night, Carlisle threatening to kill us, and what we intended to do. I told him Sam and

I wouldn't shoot first. But Sam and I would defend ourselves! Sanchez certainly wouldn't want us, his deputies, to turn tail."

"Houston, Frank. I won't let you two go alone against Carlisle and his friends. I can't move my left arm-but I can shoot with my right. We've always done everything together since we were youngers out of Georgia."

Laura's feminine but determined voice broke in. "AJ cannot go with you. He is in no condition to fight. He has only one arm and can't shoot! He can't even get out of bed!

"It's not only his arm. The Bowie cut deep into his belly and chest, almost into his heart. I don't care what you men think! He's not going to gunfight today! He simply cannot physically do it."

"Houston," I said, you two cannot go it alone against Carlisle. He's a stone cold killer! Get Sheriff Sanchez to help! Get the Monte Boys. They'll help!

"But don't let Alex go with you! He's only a saw bones. He's ridden with us Monte Boys against all sorts of banditos, even against Murrietta and Vasquez. When we caught banditos, I would pronounce 'em guilty, and the posse would hang them.

"If we didn't know them and they hadn't told us their names, Alex would chop off their heads, tied their hair around his saddle horn and packed their heads back to town, pickle the bad heads in good brandy, and leave the heads upright in jars in his library until someone identified them."

I couldn't turn my head to see who it was, but I heard footsteps coming into my room.

"Although he pronounced them dead and beheaded them, he did little shooting or fighting. He can't help you in a real gunfight.

"And Houston, again, if you have listened closely to him, his three years of Army duty in the Indian Wars did not really involve real gun slinging."

When I heard the next voice, I knew who had walked into the room.

"A.J., You don't know what you're talking about! I've never spoken of my three years of the Indian-Mexican Wars. You may have been in a few gun fights, but I've been in wars, real wars when tens of men have died in an hour and hundreds have been wounded. You small town sheriffs don't really know what a real fight is.

"At least I married the best part of your family. Bah!" And Dr. Thomas Alexander Mayes turned and walked out.

An embarrassed moment of silence ensued. Then, I continued to speak. "I'm pleased he married Mary Ann. He's a strong man and will protect her. That's what's necessary in our town.

"But despite what Alex said, he simply does not understand what it means to have a mad man like Carlisle say he'll kill you and your family.

"There is still too much small town South Carolina and New York in Alex. He's not in the Army now and he is not riding with his troops into battle. He just doesn't understand the fighting West. He cannot go into this fight.

"Carlisle will find some trick and it won't be a fair fight. He'll have Breed, Lander and his Texas friends there! They'll kill Alex! Don't let him fight our family wars!"

"AJ, relax. You can't go with us. You can't even get out of bed! Don't worry. Francis and I will take care of Carlisle and his friends. Sheriff Sanchez and Evertsen have already obtained warrants for Carlisle's arrest and there should be another warrant issued for attempting to murder you last night. We'll have Sanchez and John E. Junior with us."

"Come on, Sam. Let's call Carlisle on this and see if he's goin' to do it. He may be just another eastern braggadocio."

"Francis! Samuel! Watch out! You know he's not. He's a stone cold, merciless killer and you know it!"

They strode out of my room without saying more. My thoughts were so focused upon their safety that I did not even say 'Adios' to my only brothers, nor did I wish them well. But the moment they left, I began to worry. Would I ever see them again? Speak with them again?

I tried to stand as soon as Samuel and Francis left, but couldn't even sit up on the side of the bed. Laura pulled and jerked my bed to the window and arranged the bolsters so I could sit up, leaning against the headboard.

She sat down next to me and we held hands as we looked out the window and across Main Street into the bar of the Bella Union. I saw my brothers, Houston and Francis, walking on the west side of Main Street, peering eastward towards the bar but the sun was in their eyes.

They crossed the street and went into Lazard's store, and soon walked out into the sun, smoking Cheroots; Sheriff Sanchez came out with them and hurried off, almost running towards the Plaza.

The Banning Stagecoach had arrived and was unloading at the main entrance in front of the hotel. The Steamer Day crowd was celebrating. Men, women, and children were milling around the coach and its passengers in the street.

The noon sun was almost directly overhead. I looked down through the bar's doorway, and saw in the reflected light from our hotel and the street, the ghostly figure of Carlisle surreptitiously move and place a shotgun and short rifle behind the clothes tree at the entrance. I could see no one else, even though I knew they must be there.

Houston and Francis, leaving Lazard's, could not see Carlisle in the relative darkness of the shadows. But he was hidden just inside the entrance, and watched them in the bar mirror, a drink in one hand, his six -shooter in the other. As they paused outside the bar before entering, Carlisle turned and took a step towards the door, lifting and extending his right arm.

Laura screamed in a high pitched voice which could have shattered glass, "Watch out!" and the three men jerked their triggers involuntarily.

Carlisle fired at Houston and Francis before their eyes could accommodate to the obscurity of the bar, missed, and immediately jumped back into the darker shadows inside the doorway.

Laura continued screaming. The Steamer Day crowd heard her and the gunshot, and knew it was not a simple cowboy being exuberant and firing his gun.

Francis Marion drew his pistol and immediately went into action. He triggered his Colt .44 until the hammer fell on an empty chamber. The bar's mirror cracked in large panes, and bottles broke. Glass crashed, broke on the counter top, and fell further, shattered into smaller pieces on the stone floor.

Other shots came from inside the bar. Ricocheting bullets wailed and whined their cry of missed targets. Men and women on the street were blazed by grazing balls. Some shots went through their clothes, but fortunately only one man and no women were hit. Men, women and children screamed and scattered away from the hotel and death, as if they were a flock of chickens with their heads cut off. A horse hitched to the stagecoach was shot by an errant bullet and dropped dead in its traces; the other horses rearing and trying to run from the carnage. Suddenly the street was empty of life, except for the young magnolia tree planted in the wooden box on the boardwalk outside the bar.

From the number of shots fired, there were at least four men shooting at my brothers from inside the bar and one or two more through the windows of adjacent rooms. If I had had my rifle, I would have shot through the hotel windows in the hopes of hitting the hidden assassins.

Samuel Houston still held his fire. Carlisle was shooting from inside the bar's shadows, using the brick and thick walls for a breastwork. Samuel charged and jumped inside the door.

A .44 ball shot through his lungs, entered into the top of his right chest and passed through the tip of his left shoulder blade. He fell to the floor with his eyes forward looking, towards Carlisle.

Samuel's arms were paralyzed with shock and he couldn't raise them. Elbows on the floor, using only his right hand, he cocked his pistol and flipped the muzzle up without raising his arms. He squeezed the trigger and placed four bullets into Carlisle's chest and stomach, a tight centering that would fit on a poker card. As Carlisle staggered back against the bar, Francis rushed in with his empty pistol, grabbed Carlisle by his shirt and hit his head him again and again with the empty gun, so savagely that the barrel was bent from its frame.

Then I saw Sheriff Sanchez arrive. Although he had rushed to the

Plaza and called on the street for citizens to help, none came. Alone, he rushed inside to the combatants, grasped Francis's gun arm, pushed Carlisle back, and stood between them, ordering them to stop fighting. Carlisle, with his scalp and face bleeding from the pounding of Francis's pistol, collapsed to the floor. Francis dropped his useless pistol, turned, reached over and pulled Samuel to a sitting position with his back leaning against the inside doorframe so he would not drown in his own blood.

Dying from the gunshot wounds, Carlisle, an iron man of muscle and incredible strength, lying on the floor on his back, head crooked up against the brass foot rail and eyes looking at Francis's back, laboriously reloaded his gun. He snapped the cylinder in and shaking, aimed his pistol with both hands. He pulled the trigger once, the cartridge fired, and simultaneously, I heard another, louder shot. Carlisle's bloodied head fell and his body collapsed.

Francis, looked out the doorway, lifted Houston, and placed him gently against the doorframe, his eyes focused upon his younger brother. Then his chest erupted forward through his shirt and serape, as if it were a bubble bursting, his arms and fingers spread wide, his head snapped backwards in recoil, his knees collapsed and his body fell forward and out the door. He had just been shot in the back by a big caliber bullet.

His torso twisted and turned as he fell on his back, down on the boardwalk of an empty street; empty and without life but for the young magnolia tree in the wooden container which shaded his face. And again, gentle Francis went alone into his personal darkness, this time in the brightness of noon on a dirty, dusty street. The strong noonday sun shone down on his serape and his empty hands were clutched over his stomach as if protecting the spot where his heart popped out of his body.

And then there was a preternatural silence as if there were an ascension to heaven. No sounds were heard; neither on the street nor from the bar.

I looked through a shattered window and saw Breed holding a smoking gun. Someone ran from an adjoining card room. The Texas gunslinger and attorney for Carlisle, James H. Lander, poked his head around the corner of the billiard room at the rear. His smoking shotgun was on the floor and he was holding his bloody leg.

Drinkers in the bar picked up the dying Carlisle and placed him on the billiard table. I saw Dr. Griffin running down the street and into the bar. He just shook his head and I heard him yell to move Carlisle into a room in the Bella Union, It would never do that antagonistic combatants die in the same hotel.

I am told that Carlisle kept swearing terrible oaths against us Kings. He promised that his son would kill any Kings, women and children as well, any who were left over. He died three hours later, still unrepentant, still blasphemous.

Houston was brought dying, into the Lafayette Hotel, and placed in the room next to mine.

"Laura, I must go to Sam. Could you help me?"

Alex rushed into my room and he and Laura carried me to the room next door. If it had been necessary, I would have crawled there alone.

"Jack?"

"Yes, Sam. I'm here."

"Did Carlisle die?"

"Houston, he's dead. You got him."

"Are you sure?"

"Yes I am. I saw them carry his body out into the street," I lied. Anything to make Sam's last hour more peaceful.

"It's all right then. I'm willing to die to rid the earth of this abominable creature. Now, at least, he won't kill anyone else, nor harm another lady.

"How is Francis?"

"Houston, he has joined our father in Heaven. God is taking care of him."

Although Houston was the single person able to see who had shot Francis, he didn't say a word about the shooting, nor did we ask, hoping to preserve his energy and sanity during his last few minutes with us.

Then Dr. Gelsich rushed into the room and assisted Alex. Houston's boots were removed. Blood gushed from his chest as he was turned over. We could see the bulge under his skin by his shoulder blade where the bullet was lodged. A simple stroke of the scalpel split the skin and the slug popped out with a thud as it hit the floor, along with the splashing of blood. Fresh linen was pressed into the exit wound on his back to stop the bleeding. Then Samuel was turned over and placed sitting up in bed. Fresh linen was packed into the entrance wound. This bundle was tied tightly over and around his chest. The bleeding finally slowed to merely staining the linen.

"Gentlemen," Dr. Gelsich announced, "If putrefaction does not set in, Houston will live. He's not coughing up blood, and this means that perhaps his lungs were not perforated. I'll come back and see him tomorrow. Keep him upright in bed. Then if he bleeds, his blood will not fill his lungs and drown him. Have him take these papers of Laudanum, one paper every four hours."

I never saw nor heard of Breed again. Lander, shot in the left hip, snuck away that day to return to Texas.

This July 6th was the shortest day of the year for Francis, less than 12 hours long. But it was the longest day of the year for our family-- beginning shortly before noon on that July 6th, and lasting throughout our every waking moment of our lifetime.

We took Francis to lie in at my home on Sanchez Street that Thursday night. The following day, Friday, we buried him in our family plot on the eastern section of the Savanna Cemetery, next to our father and mother.

A week later, I read in my own newspaper, The Los Angeles Semi -Weekly Southern News, that on July 13, the Grand Jury presented an indictment against Samuel Houston King for murder. Many prominent jurists, some in writing, stated the case would not bear investigation, and that the accused was innocent.

How could this indictment happen to a good man, who was even a partner with Governor George Downey in a sheep ranch, and an elected Peace Officer in Los Angeles County? One who was assisting a Los Angeles Deputy Sheriff in arresting a wanted outlaw, an outlaw who killed a Deputy Sheriff during the arrest! What was wrong in defending oneself by shooting a murderer during his act of killing an arresting officer? And what about his attempt to kill me the night before, an Under Sheriff of Los Angeles?

Cannot one protect oneself against an enemy who has sworn to kill him? When even on his deathbed, that murderer did not repent but called upon his son to continue to kill all Kings?

Was it because of his wealth during life that he became so powerful in death? Or was this a vendetta against the southern King-Mayes family who had always supported the Californios?

Did the indictment against Houston portend the last, the total change of the Californios way of life, and mirror the present financial collapse presently occurring throughout California? Was politics "The God" above all? Was this the Northern Republicans against the Southern Democrats?

But why did we not walk away from Carlisle and let the courts handle this rogue killer? Wonderful Francis would still be with us; someone else would have arrested Carlisle.

In reflection, I must be honest with myself. My thoughts are a wail against Francis's death! Better to let a dozen Carlisles live than suffer a premature loss of one Francis. I would never again share a meal, a drink, a segar or cheroot with him. After 34 close years, to be suddenly cut out of our life, leaving us to mourn for the remainder of our earthly existence! Half of me, half of my life just disappeared. And he- without wife or children, so that we could not see his future unroll in them. Yes, I would name my next child after Francis and Sam already had a two year old son named after him. But that could not assuage the family's loss. There would always be emptiness, a darkness, even though there was light to see.

# TRIED FOR MURDER

The Court Bailiff cried, "All stand! The District Court for the City and County of Los Angeles will come to order in the Trial of Samuel Houston King for the murder of Robert S. Carlisle. In this special term, Honorable Pablo de la Guerra will preside. All will be seated."

After the seating of the twelve good men of the jury, the bailiff continued. "His Honor requests that the spittoons be used with diligence and accuracy. No one will fire his gun inside the courtroom for any reason, or the Judge and his Marshall will shoot to kill. Knives will not be drawn, even to cut plugs. This will not be like other trials in which spectators have taken over and shot at the judge or witnesses. Attorneys will not be allowed to throw inkstands; attorneys will not be allowed to place their feet on top of tables but must keep them on the floor. Those who will not abide by these rules must leave now. You have been warned!"

Jurors and spectators alike, looked at one another with surprise, muttering, "We've never heard of anything like this!"

"What is Guerra trying to do?"

Dryden, Houston's attorney, growled in a low voice that carried across the room to the jury box, "If Guerra tries that, there'll be more than one war in here." The jury snickered and some of the spectators openly laughed at Dryden's comment and these stringent, unenforceable rules.

As an attorney, I knew that in one sentence, Dryden had already created his position of dominance in the courtroom. Even sitting, Dryden was the center of attention and now owned the attraction of all in the Court.

The Honorable de la Guerra stared down at Dryden, then addressed the Court: "This is a trial of significant importance. The deceased, Robert S. Carlisle, was a man of highest regard, one of the wealthiest men in our State, a Republican known throughout our country, who provided our Union Forces with beef and tallow throughout our recent conflict.

"The accused, Samuel Houston King, is also a respected man, a Democrat who is in partnership with former Governor John G. Downey in a sheep ranch. He, too, needs to be judged fairly."

"Hear, hear." "That's right, Your Honor" came from voices in the crowded courtroom. Then other cries followed, "Sam shouldn't be here at all."

"Carlisle should have been shot years ago!"

And Dryden muttered again in a stage whisper heard throughout the courtroom, "Damn right."

Judge de la Guerra continued without allowing the cries to disturb him. "Our Trial Court will provide justice to these individuals and will not be influenced by rowdy behavior. This trial is politically significant and I intend that the recent War of Northern Aggression shall not color our jury, nor will it influence our neutral justice.

"Will the attorney for the City and County of Los Angeles, please begin the prosecution's case by making his opening argument. He will then be followed by Mr. King's attorney making an opening statement for the defense."

I was sitting in an aisle chair, in the middle of the second floor courtroom of the Clock tower Courthouse, our new courthouse purchased by the city in 1864. Little did I know when I and my fellow attorneys proposed the purchase of a single building for the ever enlarging court system that a member of my own family would stand here to be tried. The concept that Samuel Houston King would be accused of murdering Carlisle was preposterous; it was only the cry for vengeance by Carlisle's wealthy, politically influential family and friends that caused this to come to pass.

Sam, Alex, Laura and I, had discussed Sam's legal defense for months, ever since he was able to think clearly in his sick bed. We needed a vigorous defender, one who would not be intimidated by the judge nor by the court, one who would take charge of the proceedings, one who would appeal to the strong, independent members of the jury, but yet, be amenable to my directions. We spent many a night following our evening repast discussing this. And there was such an attorney in town!

Fortunately, I possessed enough monies to pay for Houston's defense and hoped it would be sufficient to counter the political significance mentioned by the judge. William G. Dryden, Esquire, was the best attorney money could buy, and he had already demonstrated his value.

The prosecutor strode confidentially to the center of the floor. "Charles H. Larrabee, Esquire, your Honor. Acting Attorney for the City and County of Los Angeles."

At this time, I was actually the Attorney for the City and County of Los Angeles but it would be a gross conflict of interest if I were to be forced to prosecute my own brother. The Grand Jury of Los Angeles had made a serious mistake in even indicting him and there would be a cloud over Houston's head and the trial itself if I were prosecuting when he would be pronounced 'not guilty.' Thus, Larrabee, an excellent attorney although a newcomer to Los Angeles, was appointed for this special term prosecution.

"Gentlemen of the jury. This is a very simple case.

"A hardened killer, a member of The Monte Boys who has been involved in many shootings and hangings, killed a leader of our community in front of innocent bystanders. It was indeed fortunate that the single death in the street was a horse, and that the other innocents only had holes shot in their clothes.

"Samuel Houston King and his brother, Francis Marion King walked to The Belle Union Hotel on that Steamer Day of Thursday, July 6, 1865 and shot and killed Robert S. Carlisle when he was innocently drinking at the bar. Don Carlisle was the owner of the Chino and the Cucamonga

Rancheros, an outstanding Californian, a pillar of our community---"

Dryden exploded out of his chair. He grasped the chair with both hands and threw it across the room at Larrabee, yelling "You lying son of a bitch! Carlisle has never been an innocent! He probably indelicately groped the mid-wife during his birth. We all know he lied and cheated every Californio he ever met, including his wife and his sister-in-law. Stick to the truth or God will smite you down and wreak his punishment upon you!

"And who made him a 'Don'? Only you, Mr. Special Prosecutor! Try proving that lie in the trial! For he certainly wasn't born as a 'Don', only as a Son of a Bitch!"

Laura, who would sit behind me throughout the trial, gasped as Dryden exploded! She had heard about Dryden's courtroom dramatics as this was one of the reasons we selected him, but she had never experienced him.

The spectators in the Court also exploded, but with cheers and applause. It was apparent they were present in order to support Sam, or at least to see the best show in town, Dryden at the bar, attacking another attorney.

Judge de la Guerra pounded his gavel so hard the handle broke. "Order in the Court!"

Both the bailiff and the Sergeant at Arms stood and peered around the courtroom, their hands on their pistols, half drawn.

"Order in the Court! Order in the Court! Mr. Dryden, sit down! Mr. Larrabee, please continue but keep to the truth. We all are aware of the dead man's reputation and it does the prosecution no good to be so disrespectful of the truth. Our blindfolded mistress of justice cannot operate well in making her decisions if her favors are sought in such a fashion."

I did not know Larrabee except in the most cursory manner as he was such a recent arrival in Los Angeles. Although he must had heard of Dryden's legendary temper and language, it is a different issue when confronted personally with a thrown chair. Yet, somehow, Mr. Larrabee was able to continue his introductory statement although his speech was somewhat hesitant. He would be a man to bear watching for the future.

I leaned forward to speak with Sam's young 21 year old wife, Jacquelina, whose entire future was dependent upon the outcome of her husband's trial. "Jacque, if this is the worst the prosecution can do, Sam will continue to eat dinner with you and your three little ones for a long time. Just let me plan and worry about this trial. Dryden and I will bring him home to you every night and we all will soon celebrate his innocence with the entire family. You should stay home with young Sam, for bringing a baby not yet one year old to Court cannot be good for him, even if it reminds the jury they have power over many people with their decision."

Larrabee continued to speak, with long pauses after each thought in his sentences. "If the brave Robert S. Carlisle had not killed Francis Marion King when he, himself, was dying, we would be trying two King brothers for murder today, not just one.

"Let no one doubt it. Samuel Houston King is a murderer and killed an outstanding member of our community. He will be, he must be, found guilty of murder!

He concluded with his opening statement; "Thank you. That is all I have to say at this time."

Judge de la Guerra looked at the 12 members of the jury as the prosecutor hurriedly sat down. "Mr. William G. Dryden will now present the opening argument for the defense. As in Mr. Larrabee's presentation, these statements are not evidence, and are not facts, but are simply what the defense will prove by means of witnesses throughout the trial."

In the short break before Dryden stood and began speaking, I leaned over and whispered to him and Houston, "De la Guerra is the judge who beat Benjamin Hayes in the judicial election last year. Probably because Hayes' court had to be recessed several times as he was so drunk that he couldn't continue to preside. Still, from Guerra's actions so far, it appears as if he does not hold our close relationship to Hayes negatively, and in fact, I detect a slight bias in our favor."

"That son of a bitch had better favor us. There is no legal reason

Houston is charged. Only the politics of a corrupt system."

After muttering this under his breath, Dryden stood and walked towards the jury box. Facing His Honor, he smiled as he stated, "Honorable William G. Dryden, Esquire, Your Honor. Defense counsel for Samuel Houston King.

He then turned so he could talk directly to the jury, and they would see every expression on his face. "Gentlemen of the jury. As the prosecutor stated, this is a very simple case.

"You have heard the District Attorney speak in simple terms, apparently reasonable. But do not forget this! This District Attorney is being paid by the county simply to convict and hang Samuel Houston King, not to seek justice.

"Did he mention that Samuel Houston King was a Deputy Sheriff seeking to arrest Carlisle? No, he did not.

"Was it mentioned that Houston's brother, Under Sheriff Andrew Jackson King, had attempted to serve a warrant upon Carlisle for fraud and theft two days earlier, and was run off the Chino Rancho by Carlisle's vaqueros at gun point? No, it was not.

"Was it mentioned that Carlisle tried to kill that same Andrew Jackson King, the City Attorney and Under Sheriff of Los Angeles on the night before the gun fight? That Carlisle stabbed him in his belly with a 15 inch Bowie knife the very night before Sheriff Samuel Houston King and Constable Francis Marion King attempted to arrest him? No, it was not.

"Was it mentioned that after stabbing Under Sheriff Andrew Jackson king, Carlisle threatened to kill all members of the King family, including women and children? No. It was not.

"Was it mentioned that Samuel's brother, Francis Marion King, whom Carlisle killed in that very same gun fight, was an elected Constable of Monte? That Francis Marion King was working under Sheriff Sanchez in assisting his brother Samuel Houston King in apprehending Carlisle, a wanted criminal? That our own Sheriff Tomas Sanchez executed a warrant to arrest Carlisle? No, none of this was mentioned.

"Carlisle was being sued under multiple law suits for fraud and theft;

stealing from his own wife and her younger sister, whose husband, John Rains, was abducted and killed stealthily and under mysterious circumstances by an supposedly unknown murderer - although one confessor has admitted that Carlisle was in the bunch who killed and mutilated John Rains.

"However, it was Carlisle who ended up owning his sister-in-law's property and suspicions are high that he was the perpetrator of the deadly deed upon her husband, John Rains. Andrew Jackson King was appointed executor of the estates in order to eliminate further thefts by Carlisle. Did the District Attorney mention this to you? No, he did not!

"Carlisle was the aggressor; he was the murderer. But Carlisle comes from an exalted, wealthy status with many politically strong Republican friends. This is the single reason that Samuel Houston King, a Democrat, whose father died as sheriff in defending our citizens of Los Angeles, and who himself lay close to death for more than half a year after trying to apprehend Carlisle, a murderous criminal, stands before you in the docket. In the name of justice, you, the jury, must find him not guilty!"

And without a break, the testimony began.

Charles Larrabee rose and hesitantly strode onto the floor.

"The prosecution calls Dr. John S. Griffen as its first witness. Please be seated in the witness chair between His Honor and the Jury."

"Dr. Griffen, did you personally know Don Robert S. Carlisle?

Dryden rose and firmly stated, "Objection by the Defense your Honor. Mr. Carlisle is not and never was a 'Don'. He arrived in California after that grand period, and was not and is not a Californio. He cannot carry that title. Defense objects to the mischaracterization and requests that he be named properly, as a Mister. The Prosecution continues to misrepresent and mischaracterize everything."

"Objection sustained. The Court rules that the decedent be named as a Mister, if an honorific be employed."

"Dr. Griffen, do you personally know Mr. Robert S. Carlisle?"

"No. I did when he was alive, but not now that he is dead."

Laughter rippled throughout the Court and continued sufficiently long to disrupt the momentum of delivery of the young prosecutor.

"Dr. Griffen, did you see the shooting which killed Mr. Carlyle?"

"No, I did not. The shooting was over by the time I got there. Carlisle had been removed from the front of the bar where the fight was and placed face up on the billiard table. He was still breathing, and with every breath was cursing at the Kings, crying out that his son would kill all of the Kings. I had him moved to a bed in the hotel. He died under my care about three hours later, at 3 o'clock, in a bed in the Bella Union Hotel."

"Did you pronounce him dead?"

"Yes I did. He stopped breathing, then he stopped bleeding. His heart had stopped."

"What was the cause of death?"

"Gunshots."

"Where was he shot?"

"Drunk, in the bar at the Bella Union Hotel."

Again, laughter from the jury and spectators broke into the rhythm the prosecutor was desperately trying to build.

"No. I meant where did the bullets hit him?"

"Two bullets had entered and remained in his chest. Another two bullets penetrated and remained in his stomach. I knew he was going to die and told him so. I tried to stop the bleeding by placing cloths on the wounds but they still oozed blood. I tried to give him Laudanum but he refused it."

"Did he tell you who shot him?"

"No sir. He did not."

"Your witness, Counselor."

Dryden turned to me and whispered, this time in a voice which would not carry further, "A.J., how should I handle the doctor? We all know he is one of the better doctors in town."

"Handle him gently. He is an honest man, a personal friend of Alex's.

He will tell the full truth unless angered, when his temper may color his judgment."

Dryden stood and moved toward the witness. "Dr. Griffen, we are friends are we not?"

"Yes Sir. I consider us friends, just as I considered Carlisle and all the Kings as friends of mine. The whole gun fight was horrible for all of us, and for our fair city as well."

"What did Carlisle tell you when you attended him for those three hours?"

"The Prosecution objects, Your Honor. That conversation obviously falls under the hearsay rule and cannot be entered into evidence."

"Your Honor. The good prosecutor himself inquired about what the decedent said. If he could do so, then it is only equal justice that the defense of Deputy Sheriff Samuel Houston King be allowed to inquire further."

"I did not so inquire!"

"Your honor, just a moment ago, the prosecutor inquired, 'Did he tell you who shot him?' and the witness responded, 'No Sir. He did not.' That is certainly such an inquiry and with an appropriate, complete answer. Justice requires that the defense be given equal access as to what was said during this critical moment"

"Objection overruled. Defense may inquire as to what was said by the dying man. Especially as the testimony indicates he had been informed by a physician that he was dying and thus unlikely to go to his Maker with lies on his lips."

"I'll repeat my query Sir. What did Carlisle tell you when he lay in his bed, dying?"

"As he lay face up, dying on the billiard table, he swore horrible oaths against the Kings. He wanted to live so he could kill them. But if he could not, then his young son would kill them. When he was moved to his chamber, he continued his cursing, horrible oaths against the Kings. He kept this up until he could no longer speak, and then he died."

"Did Carlisle mention the preparations he had made in the Bella Union Bar before the Kings arrived?"

"No Sir. He did not."

"Thank you Dr. Griffin. You're excused unless the prosecution has further questions."

"We have no further questions your Honor. Please excuse the witness."

"Your Honor, please call Thomas Sanchez, Sheriff of Los Angeles as the next witness for the prosecution."

Sheriff Sanchez rose and walked slowly and purposefully, almost ponderously, to the witness stand. It was apparent he did not wish to be called by the City Attorney to prosecute his own officer. But the citizens of Los Angeles knew him and knew his honesty. He would speak the truth, no matter what the consequences were.

"Sheriff Sanchez, you have been sworn to tell the truth. Did you speak with either Samuel Houston King or his brother, Francis Marion King on the day of the gun fight at the Belle Union Hotel?"

"I did, Sir."

"Would you please tell the Court what was said."

"Objection Your Honor. That question is a two headed rattler in a Cholla bush. No one knows where it is going and which head is speaking and we sure as Hell can't go in and chase it out!"

"Sustained. The Prosecution will reword the question so that no one will be bit, and not know by which critter."

"Sheriff Sanchez, did you meet and speak with either Houston or Francis King on the morning of July 6, 1865?"

Sheriff Sanchez spoke slowly and deliberately, delivering his words in an old Californios inflection and accent. Yet, there was no difficulty in understanding any thought spoken, although hesitations made it apparent that he translated some phrases from the Mexican before speaking.

"Yes sir, I did. I spoke with both of them at the Courthouse. They had come to town from their ranches, delivering lumber and sacks of barley for the Clear Creek Ranch. They heard about Under Sheriff Andrew Jackson lying wounded in bed because of serious cuts he received from Carlisle's Bowie the night before. My jailor, Andrew Henderson, met the brothers by their wagon. He told them that A.J. was not hurt as badly as first thought. Houston replied, 'It's not Carlisle's doing. If the Bowie hadn't struck a rib, it would have killed AJ on the spot.'

"They then came to me because they wanted to know what was being done about it. I told em, 'A warrant has been sworn out for the arrest of Carlisle because of his attack on Deputy Marshall John Evertsen the night before at the Bella Union. I did it myself. It was for 'Riotous Conduct and Resisting an Officer.' I hadn't even had time to make one up for his stabbing A.J.'

"Did you say anything to them?"

"Yes. I told em that I would find us some help and we would all go get Carlisle."

"What did you do then?"

"I went into the street and stores at The Plaza asking for help in arresting Carlisle. I would deputize anyone who was willing."

"No one wanted to help us arrest Carlisle. He was one bad hombre and he had already been drinking for hours at the hotel bar. No one wanted to help the law. They were all afraid of Carlisle and his friends."

"What did you do next?"

"I was at the Plaza and heard gunshots. I ran to the north door of the Bella Union on North Main Street where they were comin' from, and went inside. I saw Houston being driven back into the street by the bullets, coughing blood and found out later that he had been shot through the lungs. Francis Marion had fired off all his shots from his Navy Colt at Carlisle.

"When Francis ran out of bullets, I saw him rush to Carlisle, grab Carlisle's collar and pull him towards the door. He was hitting Carlisle over the head with his empty gun so hard it broke. Later, we found that the gun couldn't fire because the trigger guard had bent in from hitting

Carlisle's head. I pulled Francis off Carlisle, turned my back to the bar, and pushed Francis out the door.

"When I was doing this, Carlisle slumped to the floor and already a dead man, reloaded his gun. With his magnificence strength, Carlisle lifted his gun with both hands and fired at Francis once. The bullet shot through my coat from the back, hit Francis in the back, and killed him with that one shot. I had already pushed Francis half out the door when he was shot. He stumbled on the boardwalk, spun around and collapsed, face up at the base of the boxed magnolia tree, his serape torn open, blood gushing all over through his blown out chest and stomach, his heart pushed out into the noon air."

"Who shot Carlisle?"

"I don't know. Either Samuel Houston or Francis Marion I guess."

After a pause, Larrabee spoke again. "Thank you. That is all from the prosecution.

"Your witness, Counselor."

"Dryden," I whispered, "The Sheriff is our best witness. Sam and Francis worked for him and I am his Under Sheriff. He will protect his men if possible, especially Sam."

"Just a few questions Sheriff." Dryden got up and slowly walked toward the jurors, then turned to face Sanchez. Now, Sanchez would be directly facing the jurors when answering questions, and the jurors could see his honest face.

"Was Carlisle a peace officer?"

"No sir. He was not. Not even an attorney of the court."

"Was Samuel Houston King a peace officer?"

"Yes Sir. He was a member of the Monte Posse, a member of the Los Angeles Rangers, and an elected Constable of El Monte."

"Were you a peace officer?"

"Yes sir. I was and am the Sheriff of Los Angeles City and County."

"Was Francis Marion King a peace officer?"

"Yes Sir. He was an elected Constable of Monte."

"Was there a warrant for Carlisle's arrest on the day of the fight?"

"Yes sir. Several.

"I was attempting to gather a group of men to serve a warrant and arrest Carlisle when the shooting started. I had not yet started to write an additional warrant on Carlisle for attempted murder on Under Sheriff Andrew Jackson King as I had been in Court all morning. There were additional warrants on Carlisle for fraud and theft, because of stealing the estate of his sister-in-law, Dona Maria Merced Williams de Rains. Following my orders, Under Sheriff A.J. King, tried to serve these warrants and papers several days before the gun fight but was shot at and run off by Carlisle's vaqueros."

"Is it correct that Carlisle was a wanted criminal and an arrest was being made by two accredited peace officers assisting you at the time he was shot and killed?"

"Yes sir. It is correct."

"Did you see who actually shot Carlisle?"

"No sir. I did not. Two officers were shooting at him; Samuel Houston King and Francis Marion King. I don't know who actually shot Carlisle. There were other shots fired from the street and it may have been some of these bullets which actually hit him."

"Did you see Carlisle shoot and kill Francis Marion?"

"No sir. I did not. My back was to him. The bullet passed through my coat and killed Francis. Another inch closer, it would have killed me as well! But I don't know for a certainty who fired at us or who shot Francis. But I do know that Carlisle had friends inside the bar who were firing at the King brothers. I saw James H. Lander shooting. He was Carlisle's attorney for his land schemes and was known as a Texas gunslinger. Somehow Lander was shot in his leg and couldn't walk for a while."

"I requested that the Sheriff's Department deliver Lander as a witness today. Why is he not here?"

"I don't know. Last summer, as soon as he could travel, he left to go home to Texas and hasn't been seen since."

"Were others in the bar firing their guns?"

"Yes. I saw Breed shooting. Shots were also fired from the billiard room and one of the card rooms in the back of the bar. So other friends of Carlisle were also shooting at the Kings."

"These shots from the back of the bar. Did they hit anyone?"

"I don't know. Francis Marion was killed but I'm sure this was done by Carlisle. Samuel Houston was shot in the lungs but at that time I was standing outside on Calle Principal with my back to the bar, and I didn't see who done that. It must have come from Carlisle or from the back of the bar. Only Samuel would be able to tell who shot him and who shot Francis."

"Thank you Sheriff Sanchez. The defense has no further questions and the witness may be excused."

"Your Honor, prosecution rests. We have proven that Samuel Houston King killed Robert S. Carlisle and..."

"Objection, Your Honor. Prosecution is already presenting his final argument for the jury and we don't want to hear that God Damned mockery twice."

"Sustained. If the Prosecution has no further witness, let the Defense call their witnesses."

It came to me as a shock! We really didn't know who killed Francis Marion. No-one could definitively state, "Carlisle, or Breed, or another conspirator shot and killed Frank." There was no proof as to who killed him.

"Your Honor, the defense calls as its first witness, Deputy Marshall John R. Evertsen."

The tall, shy, fair-haired Evertson stood up and almost stumbled as he shuffled to the witness's chair. There was no force in his step. It was easy to see he had not yet become accustomed to the power inherent in his badge and his Viking forbearers had not yet exerted their inheritance.

Dryden stood, arms crossed over his chest, shoulders thrown back.

He had made the same evaluation of the witness and he was ready to supply the stamina the friendly witness lacked.

"You have been sworn in. Did you ever hear Carlisle issue threats against the lives of the King brothers?"

"Yes Sir."

"Would you please tell us when and where."

"I was on duty the night of the fifth of July. I heard a pistol shot. It appeared to come from the bar at The Bella Union Hotel. I stepped inside. Carlisle was drunk and screamin' threats against the lives of the three King brothers. That is, Andrew Jackson King, Samuel Houston King and Francis Marion King. He said he was goin' to kill them as soon as he saw them.

"I placed my hand on his shoulder and told him, 'I arrest you.' He then began swingin' his 16 inch Bowie knife, tryin to cut me up and kill me. Dr. Winston and Carlisle's vaqueros had to stop him. They finally got him into the billiard room and calmed him down. They asked me to come back in the morning and arrest him when he was sober and I agreed."

"Did you see Carlisle again?"

"No Sir. Not alive. The first thing next morning, I went to the Courthouse and got me a warrant for his arrest because of 'Riotous Conduct and Resisting an Officer'. I ran to The Bella Union when I heard shots but the shootin' was over before I arrived. Carlisle was dead on the floor before I could serve it."

"Thank you. No further questions from the Defense."

"The Prosecution has a few questions Your Honor."

"Is it true that you are related to the killer Samuel Houston King?"

Dryden half rose without really leaving his chair. "Objection from the Defense, Your Honor. No one has proved that Samuel Houston King murdered Carlisle. At worse, it appears as self-defense to me."

"Sustained. Mr. Prosecutor, please restrain from indulging in intemperate remarks, no matter how well cloaked."

"Thank you, Your Honor. I shall do so.

"I shall repeat my last inquiry. Is it true that you are related to Samuel Houston King?"

"No Sir."

"No? Do you not have a sister Laura Cecelia Evertsen? Did she not marry Andrew Jackson King on New Years Eve, December 31, 1862? Have you prevaricated throughout your entire testimony, which you swore upon a bible would be the truth?"

Dryden explosively jumped up overturning his chair that I expected would again be thrown at Larrabee. Larrabee must have thought so too as he sprang backwards and ran behind his chair at the City Attorney's table.

Dryden almost shouted at the Court, "Your Honor! We object most strongly to this attempt upon character assassination of Los Angeles's own Peace Officer. Under Sheriff A.J. King is married to the beautiful and most pleasant example of outstanding American Womanhood, Laura Evertsen King. Although the King family would be proud to recognize Deputy Marshall Evertsen as a relative, it sadly is just not true.

"But even it were true, we are sure the Deputy Marshall would uphold the honor of his professional calling, testifying to the truth, even without his issuance of the most awesome oath made upon the bible. After all, he is an agent of the prosecutor and was sent as the prosecutor's agent to arrest Carlisle."

"Objection sustained. Mr. Prosecutor. Do not further try the patience of this Court!"

Larrabee's shoulders fell and appeared to collapse together. With a hangdog, lugubrious look on his face, he responded with a decided lack of energy following Dryden's killing rejoinder with the further admonition from the court, "I apologize your Honor, both to you and the Court."

Dryden could not let that go. He had to push it further to obtain a greater psychological dominance over Larrabee. "But what about Deputy Marshall Evertsen? You can't apologize to him after that public slander?"

"Yes sir. I do apologize to Deputy Marshall Evertsen."

Evertsen stood and almost ran from the stand as Dryden began requesting, "Will the Court please call Mr. B. Phillips to the stand as the next witness."

"Mr. Phillips, did you live at the Bella Union Hotel during July of 1865?"

"Yes, I did. I still do."

"On the morning of July 6 of last year, did you speak with Carlisle?"

"Yes Sir, I did. I walked down to the bar about 8 o'clock for a drink. Carlisle and his gun shootin lawyer, Lander, were sittin at the table by the archway that lead to the new outside closets. From the whiskey they'd drunk, they'd been there for hours. Carlisle came over to me askin, 'Do you still have that shotgun you borrowed from me a month ago?' 'Yes Sir, I said.' He then told me, 'Get it quick, and make sure it's Damn well filled with the big load for huntin deer.'

"I went and got the shotgun but had no charges. I went next door to Lazard's Store and got about 12 buck loads. Then I laid in a load of powder in the hole. It was primed to shoot.

"I went back to Carlisle. He was one scary man! He said, 'Put the shotgun behind the door by the writing desk.' I did it and got outa there! I was so scared of him, I didn't ask fir the good money I had paid."

"Did you speak with him again?"

"No Sir. The next time I saw him, he was dead on the billiard table."

"Did Carlisle fire that shotgun?"

"No, he didn't. Guess he was too busy firin his other guns."

"Did you find the broken gun of Francis Marion?"

"Yes sir, I did. I gave it to the court at the beginning of this here trial."

"Thank you. That's all. You're dismissed."

I knew I would be called next as Dryden and I had discussed my testimony last night. As an officer of the Court, I must tell the truth. But only to the question put to me. As I had counseled so many of my clients, testify to the truth, but do not volunteer any information. That would only break up the planned presentation of your attorney and lead to further questioning by your opponent. In my case, it might prove disastrous to Sam. Even Dryden was unaware that I had seen the gunfight from my window across the street. All were in belief I had lain there, unconscious, flat on my back. I need not inform Dryden of everything, in particular that which might well destroy the defense of his client and I didn't.

"Defense will now call Under Sheriff Andrew Jackson King."

I got up, walked to the witness chair and sat down. Dryden and I had prepared this well. Not only was I the defendant's brother, but I was the Under Sheriff and the City and County Attorney for Los Angeles as well. I must make a good, honest impression.

"You have sworn on a          bible that you would tell the truth. Despite the fact that Samuel

Houston King is your brother, are you sure you will testify only the truth? I'm asking this so Mr. Larrabee will believe you and won't ask it again."

"Samuel Houston King is--"

"Objection, Your Honor. - "

"Mr.Larrabee. Sit down or I'll adjourn the Court, bodily throw you out, and then reconvene! Don't waste our time! We all know how you challenged Deputy Marshall Evertsen, so forget this and don't try it again."

"Samuel Houston King is my brother and I want to, and will speak to the truth about his shooting. He laid home in bed for longer than six months, fortunately recovering from being shot through his lungs when most men would have died. Now he must face this mockery of a trial process only because of Carlisle and his fine Republican friends who stole over 46,000 acres of prime ranch land from our Californio friends. We all know the reason why Houston is on trial and it's not because of the shooting."

Judge de la Guerra interrupted. "Sheriff King. Please respond only to the questions put to you and do not volunteer other information."

"Yes Sir, Your Honor."

Dryden now continued. "I'll just ask a few questions. Is Samuel Houston King your brother?"

"Yes Sir. He's my younger brother."

"Did you hear Carlisle threaten you or your brothers?"

"Yes, I did. On the night before the gun fight, the night of Mr. Solomon Lazard's wedding, Carlisle was drunk as usual. He tried to kill me by cutting me with his 16 inch Bowie knife. When he was stabbing me, he yelled out, 'And I'm going to kill your brothers too. Tell them I'm going to kill all the Kings. Meet me at noon down in the bar here.' He screamed this to the crowd at the wedding ball at the Bella Union Hotel. He had carved me up in the chest and arm, and thought he had stabbed me in the heart. He believed I was dead or at least wouldn't live."

"Did you tell this to your brothers?"

"Yes Sir, I did. The next morning when they visited me at The Lafayette Hotel. I don't remember the particulars, but we had learned that Carlisle wanted a fight a little before 1200, so he and his friends could catch the Banning Stage at noon to the harbor, sailing on the *Senator* for San Francisco until things quieted down."

"So your brothers, Constables Francis Marion King and Samuel Houston King were aware that Carlisle was setting a trap for them?"

"Yes sir, we all knew that. Carlisle had never fought fair in his life."

"Thank you, that is all unless the Prosecutor has further questions."

"Just one, Your Honor."

"Earlier, there was testimony that the Bowie knife was only 15 inches long. Why do you now claim it is 16?"

"Counselor, at the time it looked as if it were 20 inches long. I was just trying to live. Someone must have actually measured it and told me in the past six months."

"The Prosecution rests, Your Honor."

"The defense now rests. We have no further witnesses."

"The trial will now recess until tomorrow morning when the attorneys will begin their final arguments." And the gavel pounded for the closure of the third day of trial.

That night, we had a grand dinner at our home in town, the Sanchez House. Our two story adobe home on Sanchez Street was just around the corner from Pio Pico's adobe on the Paseo de la Plaza and was one of the three structures at the Plaza to have a red tile roof made in the old Spanish way, soft clay bent over the knee of a workman and around his thigh, and then dried in the sun. Memories are so short that almost all had forgotten that originally the house and street had belonged to the Sanchez Californios and that this had been their town home away from their Rancheros. Sheriff Tomas Sanchez was a member of that family.

It was a large dinner gathering, the first one there since our brother Francis Marion had been laid out on that fateful day of July 6, 1865. It was celebratory, yet somber, as all adults were aware of the possible danger under which Samuel still lingered. It was my position as eldest and most legally experienced, as well as the host, to set the tone of the dinner.

I gently rang the bell of my goblet with the blade of my knife which produced a clear light undulating mellow tinkling, and all stopped talking. "Ladies and Gentlemen. Please charge your glasses. I propose a toast tonight, first in honor of our fallen brother, Francis Marion." Gayety fell silent, as all remembered the eldest of our generation and the shortest day of his life.

After a moment of silence, I again spoke. "Please recharge your glasses. I now propose a toast to Samuel Houston, victorious in battle, who won a decisive victory today, and who will be victorious in the Court Room tomorrow." The sounds of congratulations and joy reached such vigor that Jacquelina had to go upstairs to breast feed little Sam Houston to stop his crying and to quiet Martha and Francis Marion. Laura stopped her hostess duties in order to quiet our little Carrol and Laura Morin. Alex and Mary Ann were not present as El Monte was quite a ride for a busy doctor and his family. Our celebration and dinner did not tarry late as tomorrow would be another enduring day and it was uncomfortable to sleep the two families in our Plaza House. Early rising is always an impediment against a late evening.

Despite my joviality during our dinner, my private thoughts kept me awake and thinking throughout the night. I know the fickleness of men, the way a jury will inexplicably produce a verdict without reason. We appeared to have decisively won against the prosecutions best work. But it was still a very dangerous world for Sam. No one knows what will happen within our city tonight which could overturn all our good lawyering.

Still as I rose in the morning, I shaved closely and dressed with special care, wearing a clean shirt and a new waistcoat. I made certain that Sam did as well.

Court began in the morning when the bailiff again announced, "All stand. The District Court for the City and County of Los Angeles will come to order in the Trial of Samuel Houston King for the murder of Robert S. Carlisle. In this special term, Honorable Pablo de la Guerra will preside. All will now be seated."

His Honor then spoke. "Already this has been a lengthy trial of three days given solely to the presentation of evidence by more than 30 witnesses. Let us conclude these proceedings as quickly as possible. Mr. Prosecutor, begin with your final argument."

"Thank you, your Honor.

"As I began three days ago, I again begin by stating this is a very simple case. A hardened shooter and his brother came to town to kill an outstanding member of our community, Robert S. Carlisle, a son of Virginia, the mother of our fair nation. Today, that murderer stands before us and must atone for his deed, just as Cain stood before his maker after he slew Abel. We have that same awesome duty to perform, and you, the gentlemen of the jury, have sworn to do so.

"Robert S. Carlisle was a Gente de Raisen, married to Francisca Williams, the granddaughter of Don Antonio Maria Lugo who's father walked with the Pobladores to found our new city, and the daughter of Don Julian de Williams. They had three children, a son and two daughters, who now must go through life separated from their father's loving arms. His sister-in-law, Dona Maria Lugo Rains is now without succor, as her husband was killed by desperadoes several years ago. The depravity of King's act can be easily seen.

"Robert S. Carlisle was an outstanding citizen of our country. Everyone must admit that during our crisis between the Northern and Southern States, he sold our Union brothers beef and hides at a fair price. He did not take advantage of our country in her direst hour. And he did his best to secure our boundaries to the East from the deprivations of war.

"But what of the depraved killer, Samuel Houston King? He plotted with his brothers to murder Don Roberto Carlisle. They had deliberately planned to meet in front of The Bella Union Hotel and together, assault and murder Don Roberto Carlisle! They entered through that north door on Main Street and started shooting. And indeed, did kill Mr. Carlisle. Have no doubt, they killed him! Samuel Houston King did kill him."

"But why did they do this? What reason?

"Thoughts have been expressed that it was over a woman. But this was a good husband and father who was shot and killed. He was not involved with another. Such is mere fabrication. Carlisle was a good man in every way."

There was so much nonsense of this type spoken by the Prosecutor that I really dozed away the day, only half-hearing his arguments, then awakening fully when His Honor terminated the proceedings in the late afternoon, stating that on the morrow, Friday, the Defense would begin its final argument.

On Friday, February 2, 1866, the bailiff opened the proceedings, followed by Judge de la Guerra's remarks. Then Defense Counsel, William G. Dryden began his final argument.

He stood and moved to his left. Standing behind Houston's chair at the defense table, he placed his hands on Houston's shoulders, a loving father protecting his son.

"Gentlemen of the jury. Making my introductory statement at the beginning of this trial, I, too, said 'This is a very simple case.'

"The prosecutor began by again naming Carlisle as a Don, a statement we objected to and which the Court stated was an untruth. I would suggest that the jury carefully note this and consider that of all the prosecutor's statements have the same lack of veracity.

"First, and mark this well! As you have heard throughout the trial, testimony from actual participants in the gun fight absolutely prove the innocence of Samuel Houston King! No one has testified that Samuel Houston King was the person who shot and killed Carlisle! No one knows who did it! It was described how shots were fired by both Samuel Houston and Francis Marion-and Francis Marion was the closest and fired the most shots, emptying his gun. Perhaps he killed Carlisle! But remember, Deputy Marshall John Evertsen heard shots being fired from Main Street into the bar of The Bella Union Hotel. These could have been the bullets that actually killed Carlisle. No one knows who fired the bullets that killed Carlisle!

"Second, and again, mark this well! Let me remind you--Carlisle was a wanted criminal. Just three days earlier, he used force to evade warrants for his arrest for fraud, theft, and unlawful sale of properties not his own, for selling of properties belonging to his sister-in-law, Dona Maria Merced Lugo Williams du Rains! He was a criminal, wanted on these warrants and had evaded their service through the use of armed force."

"Our Los Angeles Sheriffs and Constables were there to apprehend and arrest this wanted criminal. Carlisle fired first, from the unseen darkness of the bar where he was lying in wait. Fired at those unsuspecting peace officers in the noonday sun, walking toward him.

"But wait. Third, and again mark this well! Other warrants were drawn at the Courthouse that very morning for Carlisle's arrest on Riotous Conduct and Resisting an Officer. And Deputy Marshall Evertsen was rushing to serve them.

"Were these the only warrants? Yes, they were the only written warrants. There was still the unwritten warrant of Attempted Murder on Under Sheriff Andrew Jackson King. And you have heard how evidence was being gathered on the unsolved murders of John Rains, Carlisle's brother-in-law and Juan Carrillo, range foreman of Dona Maria Merced Williams du Rains' Cucamonga Ranch. We cannot say why Carlisle was not held to account, when witnesses have stated he was involved. But we do know that the killing of these men allowed Carlisle to snake his way into the executorships of the estates, falsify documents and fraudulently sell his wife's and sister-in-law's properties.

"Fourth-yes there is a fourth-an unarguable reason for the innocence of Sheriff Samuel King! He was a Peace Officer, an elected constable from El Monte, also in Los Angeles County, as well as a member of the Los Angeles Rangers. He was on official business, assisting Sheriff Tomas Sanchez in the arrest of Carlisle, when on that very day, other citizens ran and hid from their civic duty. Shall we, should we, arrest and hold liable our own officers when they are fulfilling their sworn duties in the presence of deadly bullets?

"You have been told how Carlisle was such a good citizen selling beef and hides to the Union States during the recent War of Northern Aggression. But did you know he sold beef and hides to our Southern States? Admittedly, both sides were sold these goods at reasonable prices. But don't believe that he was a patriot in any manner! He was a business man as well as a thief. And who knows, perhaps he also sold your cattle that remain missing. After all, he stole cattle from his wife and her sister and sold them!

"Samuel Houston King is a hero, not a criminal. We should be crying 'Hosanna' to the Heavens because of his heroic deeds, not trying him. He and his brother Francis have had their good names vilified by our corrupt political system. The politicians have caused an innocent man to be brought to trial, and we, in this court, have the power to rectify that abominable, misbegotten, lawless deed!

"Gentlemen of the Jury, Samuel Houston is innocent and you must find him Not Guilty!

"Thank you for your presence and performance of your duty as jurors."

Judge de la Guerra addressed the Court. "It is Friday evening. The Court will now adjourn. I shall take the unusual procedure and convene the Court tomorrow morning, Saturday, at 900 AM. The Jury will begin its deliberations at that time. Please arrive timely."

On Saturday, February 3, the Court convened at 900 AM. The case was delivered to the Jury for its deliberations.

As the Jury left its box, I leaned over and shook Houston's hands. "Good luck." Then I leaned around Dryden and hugged my sole surviving brother. They couldn't fault Houston for what he did or actually, for what he did not do.

When I again spoke, it was with assurance and with no doubt in my voice. Houston needed all his strength now. "If the Jury returns soon, it's always a sign of acquittal. It means they have all agreed on the facts and made the decision unanimously. Let's hope we can eat supper at home this midday. Would you enjoy a good beef steak? I'll ask Laura to prepare four rare ones. She's been hanging a side above the cooling stream for a week now."

But silence soon crept in. There was little to talk about. Our thoughts were elsewhere, and private. I again thought of Francis, going alone into his dark. Is there a God? Would we see Francis in the afterlife again? Speak with him, enjoy his laughter? What was life really about? Does what we do really make a difference in the world of man? Or would we simply be replaced by another, and be subjected to his whims? Earlier, Sam had named a son Francis Marion but would he be my brother, my friend of 34 years? Would hanging our Sam be similar to hanging a beef in God's eye?

Suddenly, at 11 AM, the Bailiff returned, strode to the Judge's office, knocked and entered. Did this mean the Jury had decided Houston's fate already? We now sat straight in our chairs.

The Bailiff soon returned, walked through the Courtroom and returned to the deliberation room. Those of us in the Court relaxed. Then he quickly returned with the jury! They had made a decision!

"All stand," he cried. "The District Court for the City and County of Los Angeles will come to order in the Trial of Samuel Houston King for the murder of Robert S. Carlisle, Honorable Pablo de la Guerra presiding."

As the Honorable de la Guerra took his seat, the bailiff further announced, "All will be seated."

His Honor inquired, "Has the Jury come to a decision in this case?"

"Yes, Your Honor," responded the Bailiff.

"Will the foreman of the Jury step forward and deliver the verdict."

Sam, Dryden, and I closely observed the foreman. He looked downbeat, somber, as did the jurors. None of them were smiling, nor were they looking at one another. Just down at the floor. Did the fickle Gods turn against Sam once again? Laura appeared as if she were breaking into tears.

The foreman, a rancher from La Nopalera, stood, squared his shoulders and firmly stepped toward the witness's chair. He looked around the Courtroom, then directly at Houston, then away from him. He pulled out his kerchief, blew into it, put it back into his pocket. Without again looking at Houston, he carefully lowered his eyes and slowly read each word aloud, "Your Honor, we find Samuel Houston King not guilty of all charges."

With that announcement, hats were thrown in the air, there were loud whoops from the crowd, hands pounded on the chairs and railings, boots stomped rhythmically on the good pine floors and some shots were fired into the ceiling of the Court Room. But now, the Judge didn't care for he had left his chair and had disappeared into his chamber. The defendant's table was overwhelmed with well-wishers, including all members of the jury.

"It was a political charge from the beginning."

"Those Damned Republicans are still trying to kill us off."

"You're a hero and should have been rewarded."

"Thank God, someone finally killed that murderer."

"Sam, let's go for a drink at the Bella."

Upon hearing the verdict of the jury, my legs began shaking imperceptibly, their movement dampened by my weight and hidden by my pants and high boots. I bent over slightly, placing my hands on the back of Houston's chair in front of me so their trembling would not be disclosed. My countenance presented the same calm, unconcerned composure it presented throughout the trial. But I could not speak. I opened my whisky bottle and slowly took a few sips. Then I turned to my good friend Dryden, of whom it was said had an extremely limited knowledge of the law but whose profanity was unlimited. "Sir, I thank you kindly for the justice served in this court today."

Dryden responded, "Your thanks are not as appreciated as much as the sack of gold doubloons you gave me. But justice has been served, even if expensively."

The celebration continued with the jury spilling out onto the floor and congratulating Sam. The spectators inside the Courtroom and even those who had stood in the hallway pushed their way down to the defendant's seat. They even pushed aside Jacque and Laura who were denied the pleasure of celebrating with their men. Everyone was pleased by the verdict. As the news spread outside, gunshots and loud cowboy yells were heard.

Finally, Houston was released by the crowd and we went to the door of the Courthouse. We just stood there and looked out. The courtyard and streets were filled with armed citizens. Cheers and cries vibrated around the Courthouse when they saw Sam; pistols and rifles were fired into the air. At least 200 vigilantes were in the crowd, heavily armed and on horseback, celebrating Houston's victory. They had gathered at the courthouse to storm it and to free Houston if the verdict had been "Guilty." I had to use my kerchief as my eyes were tearing from emotion.

That noon, my house was filled with friends celebrating. I, too, was celebrating for Houston. But where was Francis Marion? And what pleasures could we have without him?

Is he out in the void, alone, and knows not of us? Again, I cry at night when I feel his loneliness.

Fortunately, Laura is with me. But who is with Francis?

# EPILOGUE

It has always been our custom to kill anyone who has killed a member of our family. A few years after the trial, as soon as Samuel Houston could make arrangements, he loaded his wife and babies into a double ox wagon, hitched six Californian range horses to it, and left in March of 1873 for Texas. His purpose was to find Lander, the gun-slinging friend of Carlisle.

Although I was the only one he told, he had seen Lander shoot Francis in the back with a shotgun. Years later, word returned to Los Angeles that Lander had been gunned down. No further information was received about the gunfight and Houston never said a word about Texas.

After Texas, Houston went into business in Arizona. He eventually continued in ranching. He, too, is buried in an unmarked grave in our family plot, next to Francis's unmarked grave. When my time comes, I hope to lie next to my brothers, unnamed and unmarked as they. The family has been keeping this site open for years. It is my wish.

# HISTORICAL FIGURES

## *Andrew Jackson King*

AJ's life changed significantly following the death of Francis Marion and the trial of Samuel Houston. He became a more temperate man and his "family" concept expanded beyond his brothers. AJ is remembered by his expanded family as selling 40 acres of apple grove to pay for the wood in his niece's (Victoria) house in El Monte and even today, more than one hundred years later, is known within the family as "Uncle Jack". He was one of the founders and investors in The Los Angeles City Water Company, to replace the Zanja Madre and to expand the water system for Los Angeles. There was also an interesting but unfortunate investment in the production of electric power from ocean waters.

In 1859, he was elected to the State Assembly and was a member of the Assembly committee which established Sacramento as the State's Capitol. In 1865, he was one of the founders and editors of the first daily newspaper published in Los Angeles County, the Los Angeles Daily News. In 1871, he was one of the founders of the County Agricultural Society. In 1873, his company published the First City Directory Of Los

Angeles.

In 1868, Governor H.H. Haight appointed him County Judge of
Los Angeles to complete the term of his old friend, William G. Dryden.
Ever seeking the elusive justice, Judge King sought to stem the vigilantes
during the Chinese massacre of October 24, 1871 with Sheriff Burns,
Judge Widney, City Attorney Cameron Thom and others, but while
girding on his guns, shot off a finger on his left hand and was unable
to muster with his friends. At the time of his death, October 14, 1923,
he was the oldest member of the Los Angeles County Bar, of which he
was one of the founders. His personal law books formed the basis of
the library of the Los Angeles Bar Association. He was survived by two
sons and two daughters; his eldest son Carrol practiced law with him.
Although it is believed that there is a present direct descendent through
Carrol King, she cannot be located. There are no known descendants of
his other children.

## Laura Evertsen King

Laura is well known to historians as she published descriptions of
early California life and personalities in the annuals of the *Historical Society
of Southern California* as well as in the *Los Angeles Times Magazine* and *The
Grizzly Bear*. This book's description of her long journey to Los Angeles
in 1849 is factual.

Laura's descriptions of early California life and customs date from
that time period although she focused her legends and folk tales on eye
witness accounts on the pre-American period. Her daughter, Laura Morin
King, was known as a water colorist of florals, and was trained at The
Los Angeles School of Art and Design with Mrs. Garden MacLeod. AJ
was very much in love with Laura until his death. She died at their home
on Breed Street February 25, 1925, after living in Los Angeles for 75
years. She may well be a more important historical personage than AJ.

## Samuel Houston King

Sam and Jacqualina had five children, three of whom had issue with a large number of descendents today. Their oldest son, who was two at the time of the gun-fight, Francis Marion King, became a well-known western figure and writer. He wrote four books on the old west.

## Francis Marion King

Francis was the oldest of the King brothers. He died in the duel, and without issue.

## Robert S. Carlisle

Carlisle's son did not attempt retribution for his father's death. Carlisle's last direct descendent died in the 1960's of old age. The most striking event regarding Carlisle following the gun-fight, occurred many years after his death back in 1865. In December of 1933, unknown vandals broke into his tomb on Fort Moore Hill, and entered the vault. Police were unable to identify the perpetrators and could not state if any object was stolen.

## Micajah Johnson

Micajah's death left five young daughters orphans. They were brought up in Lexington, which was later renamed as part of El Monte, by other Johnsons (not necessarily members of the same family). All married at a young age. Many of the streets in present day El Monte are named after these founding families.

Descendants of Micajah and the Kings are friends today, bound together by history and their common tragedy. Family records document that both families lived in Sante Fe, New Mexico from 1849 until 1852, and it is assumed that in this small town, they knew one another. In 1852, both families left in different wagon trains for the "Trail's End" at the San Gabriel River in El Monte/Alhambra. Descendents of the Kings and of Micajah are buried in the Savannah Cemetery in Rosemead, California, although in different family plots.

## Thomas Alexander Mayes

In 1852, Dr. Mayes was the only physician in Los Angeles County who was a graduate of a formal medical school, Jefferson Medical College in Philadelphia. Following graduation, he practiced in New York. After a year, he and two fellow physicians joined the U.S. Army and were sent to the West to serve in cavalry units. While in Sante Fe, New Mexico, he met and fell in love with Miss Mary Ann King, older sister of the King brothers. Despite rejection of his proposal of marriage, Dr. Mayes resigned his commission and followed her wagon train to "Trail's End" at the San Gabriel River in 1852.

Mary Ann married him after further courtship, perhaps because in 1853, he built the first wooden house in Lexington (El Monte) for her; two stories with a porch and a balcony on the second floor. He and Mary Ann lived their entire life in that house on South Lexington Avenue, raising five children to adulthood. Dr. Mayes served twice as Los Angeles County Coroner; 1854 and 1855.

There is a strong line of descendants. Politically, Dr. Mayes was an influential democrat, a trustee of the school board and was elected Los Angeles County Coroner, a position he served for many years. He and his immediate descendants are buried in the family plot (King, Mayes, Haddox) at the Savannah Cemetery.

## District Court for the City and County of Los Angeles, 1866

The description of the courtroom antics of the attorneys, witnesses, and spectators appears incredible. But when one reads about those early days of the infant Los Angeles Judicial System, the Kafkaesque trial of Samuel Houston King lies well within the factual range. After all, there were no schools of law here, and frequently, admission to the Bar was simply a trip to the Bella Union Hotel with a handshake and drink to celebrate. Interested parties are referred to *Lawyers of Los Angeles* published by the Los Angeles Bar Association in 1959, even as to the descriptions of Judges Dryden and Hayes.

Although a published statement made by the Director of Public Information, Superior Court, Los Angeles County, indicates all records and trial documents were transferred to *The Huntington Library*, a personal search of all legal documents (round files) of that era fails to disclose any record of the trial, even as to the fact that the trial occurred. Fortunately, a newspaper (owned by AJ!) recorded Sam's acquitance along with a brief description of the trial.

Official notes at the Huntington Library entitled *"from the courts,"* list civil cases citing Carlisle as defendant and listing amongst others, A.J. King acting for the accusers, as *"missing."* Other records are not to be found; some are notated as *"returned to the Hall of Records,"* but a search in those subterranean realms again failed to disclose such records.

## Don Pablo de la Guerra

A Californio, defeated Judge Benjamin I. Hayes in an election and began serving the Court on January 1, 1864. He is rated as one of the better judges and is praised for his decisions.

## Benjamin Ignatius Hayes

Judge Hayes is noted as an early jurist and is described as "one of California's most brilliant legal minds." His diaries and scrapbooks are an important source of information of the early history of Los Angeles and Southern California. A partial collection from his diaries and letters was published as *Pioneer Notes* in 1929. More than 100 of his written collections have survived and are in the *H.H. Bancroft Collection.* He had one child who grew to adulthood, John Chauncey Hayes, who served as a judge for many years in Oceanside, California.

# ABOUT THE AUTHOR

**Victor Gilmore Haddox, MD, JD**, served with the United States Marine Corps (Cpl) during WW II and was again activated for 11 months in the United States Army Reserve (COL) during Desert Shield/Desert Storm. As a young student, he hitchhiked through Turkey and Persia. As an adult, he has slept on Arctic snow in minus 45-degree weather without a shelter, and dry camped during high summer in Death Valley. He is a Clinical Professor of Psychiatry and the Behavioral Sciences at the at the University of Southern California, Keck School of Medicine, Institute of Psychiatry and the Law. His family settled in the Los Angeles area in 1849 and played a minor but significant role in the development of Los Angeles and California.